Reviews on *Because of a Boy*

"Remarkably realistic characters
and a fast-paced story make Anna DeStefano's
Because of a Boy hard to put down."
—*Romantic Times BOOKreviews*

"An emotional story that forces her characters
to trust based on gut feeling, and this left this
reader in tears more than once."
—*LovesRomanceandMore.com*

"A page-turning read."
—*BooksForABuck.com*

"Totally engrossing…a winning start."
—*Cataromance.com*

Dear Reader,

ATLANTA HEROES has been such a fun series to write. With each new story I find myself fascinated with not just the hero and heroine, but with their friends and family, too. Every character jumps off the page for me. In last fall's *Because of a Boy,* it was Robert Livingston who kept insisting that he had an amazing story of his own to tell. And man, does *To Protect the Child* start off with a bang!

Robert, a high-profile neurosurgeon, faces life and death on the job every day, so it's only natural that it would take another adrenaline junkie to snag his attention. Only, he doesn't realize who he's dealing with when Alexa Vega is wheeled into his O.R.—she has amnesia and remembers nothing about the violent confrontation that left her with severe head trauma. But there's something in Alexa's drive to keep fighting in the midst of the nightmares that haunt her, and to protect a mysterious child no one knows anything about, that speaks to Robert.

I love exploring the suspense and passion that every ATLANTA HEROES story deserves. I hope you're enjoying the new twists and turns, as well. Please let me know what you think of ATLANTA HEROES at www.annawrites.com. And join the fun and fabulous giveaways at annadestefano.blogspot.com.

Oh, and don't forget to come back later in the year to catch up with Rick Downing's story!

Sincerely,

Anna DeStefano

TO PROTECT THE CHILD
Anna DeStefano

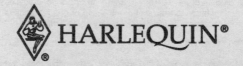

HARLEQUIN®

TORONTO • NEW YORK • LONDON
AMSTERDAM • PARIS • SYDNEY • HAMBURG
STOCKHOLM • ATHENS • TOKYO • MILAN • MADRID
PRAGUE • WARSAW • BUDAPEST • AUCKLAND

ISBN-13: 978-0-373-71497-1
ISBN-10:   0-373-71497-1

TO PROTECT THE CHILD

www.eHarlequin.com

Printed in U.S.A.

ABOUT THE AUTHOR

Romantic Times BOOKreviews award-winning author Anna DeStefano volunteers in the fields of grief recovery and crisis care. The rewards of walking with people through life's difficulties are never-ending, as are the insights Anna has gained into what's most beautiful about the human spirit. She sees heroes everywhere she looks now. The number one life lesson she's learned? Figure out what someone truly needs, become the one thing no one else could be for that person and you'll be a hero, too!

Books by Anna DeStefano

HARLEQUIN SUPERROMANCE

Don't miss any of our special offers. Write to us at the following address for information on our newest releases.

Harlequin Reader Service
U.S.: 3010 Walden Ave., P.O. Box 1325, Buffalo, NY 14269
Canadian: P.O. Box 609, Fort Erie, Ont. L2A 5X3

For those everywhere
who see beyond their lives
and become
another's hero.

CHAPTER ONE

"MOVE!" SHE WHISPERED as loud as she dared. "It's going to be okay. I promise. But we have to move."

Just a little farther away from the building. Down the alley, to the street, and then...

Then what?

There was no *little farther.* No *safe.* Not until they were miles away. Too bad her escape plan was more of a shot in the dark than an actual plan.

There were shadows flanking the street entrance to the long alley. Human shadows she wasn't sure were friend or foe.

"Quick, back here." She cut behind one of the Dumpsters beside the door they'd escaped through.

He'd be furious.

Deadly furious.

She could hear them searching inside the warehouse. Frantic. And they never bothered to be frantic, except when following orders or covering their asses. So much for her element of surprise.

Shouts echoed. Their hide-and-seek posse was about to spill outside.

"Lexi?" The whisper at her elbow was shaky. Terrified.

"Shh." She squeezed the sweaty palm clinging to hers.

It was midday, but her warning hung like a hazy omen in the cold air. Just breathing could get them caught.

"We have to be quiet," she warned.

It was either be quiet or be dead. And dead wasn't going to happen.

She could still make this disaster right.

Somehow.

She glanced toward the street. Still no movement. Maybe no threat. But she had to be sure.

The shadows and filth around them revealed no makeshift weapons. No epiphanies for how to fix this.

"Lexi, I dropped Felix in the warehouse. I have to—"

"What!"

Damn!

"I have to go back for him." The hand tugged free. "I have to—"

"We can't go back!"

No Felix.

No gun.

She had no business trying to do this on her own. But there'd been no time. And now everything was unraveling, and she didn't have a choice….

"But—"

"No!"

Worry about Felix later. Get to later first.

They had to reach the street while there was still time, then—

The door creaked open, hinges scraping, rust against rust. Footsteps left the warehouse and echoed across the damp concrete, scuffing against discarded cardboard, scattering the junk littering the ground.

She forced shallow breaths. One hand motioned for silence, the other pressed against the pitted surface of the Dumpster. It was too obvious a hiding place.

As if she'd had tons of alternatives!

Desperation makes you reckless, a voice from her past had once cautioned. *But you can use the recklessness to your advantage.... Every now and then, you'll make yourself a little luck.*

The footsteps stopped.

The Dumpster's lid lifted long enough for someone to peer inside, then it slammed shut. Hard-soled shoes shuffled in opposite directions. Two sets of them, heading toward either side of the bin.

Screw luck.

"Run!" She shoved against the Dumpster, crashing it into the men. "Run to the street and don't look back! Help! Help us!"

Grunts.

Curses.

One of the men hit the ground, his gun skidding away. She grabbed it and sprung from her crouch into a full sprint. More footsteps poured into the alley from the warehouse.

"Help us!" she yelled again.

The shadows down the alley turned, bodies in motion heading their way. Not friends after all.

She raised the gun.

Trying to shoot her way out was stupid. There were too many of them. But stupid wasn't dead.

They still had a chance, as long as—

A hand clenched in her hair and yanked her backward.

"No!" She kicked as she was dragged away from the street. "Run! Whatever you do, don't stop running!"

She twisted to face her attacker. Ignored the pain. She brought the gun around to fire, knowing she was already done. But there was done, and then there was taking one of these bastards with her.

She had a sudden taste for the latter.

She'd distract them for a few more seconds, then—

"Lexi!" The terrified scream came from the street.

A shadow closed in from behind her. Before she could react, the side of her head exploded in pain.

She crumpled to the ground, taking her attacker down, too. Failure echoed around her—more screams for help, bouncing off the buildings around them. Blackness enveloped her. An automatic pointed between her eyes, pressed to her forehead.

"You stupid bitch," a disembodied voice growled.

The child's next scream ripped through her pain. Along with it came the certainty that it was almost over.

It was finally over.

"Do it," she snarled, the weakest part of her relieved as the alley faded to black.

But the nightmare continued, and in it, she kept fighting…. Kicked to get free…

Twisted against her restraints…

Strained against the hands holding her to the table…

Fought the pain and the light shattering her skull…

Table?

Light?

The blackness shifted to gray…. Reality drawing closer…

"Hold her still," a soothing voice commanded.

The warm hand on her shoulder belonged to the voice, not the icy cold of her nightmare. It was soft, not cruel, absorbing her shivers. Quieting them.

"It's okay," he whispered near her ear. "Try to relax. You're safe now."

She somehow willed her body to still and her eyes to open. A tall figure towered over her.

Blue, shapeless shirt.

Blue mask.

Bluer eyes.

Honest eyes.

Safe.

Her mind recoiled from the thought. She tried to jerk away from the gentle touch, but he stopped her. Him and the heaviness stealing through her body.

He smiled behind his mask, his expression kind.

Caring. She hadn't wanted either from anyone in a long time. She was certain of it, even though nothing else made sense.

"We've given you a sedative," he explained. "You should be starting to feel it. Try to relax. No one's going to hurt you here."

Her instinctive laugh escaped as a moan.

He studied the whirring and beeping monitors she hadn't noticed before. His hand moved to the bandage she suddenly realized engulfed half her head, pulling it back to check beneath.

"You've got one minute to get her under," he instructed someone she couldn't see.

The blackness reached for her again.

His fingers smoothed down her cheek, easing her panic. More effective than any drug. She blinked against the shadows, needing to see his eyes a while longer. Their blue was shot through with a steely, determined gray.

"Help me," she begged. "You have to help me get out of here. Get to the street. We need to go…."

"What street?" he asked. "*We* who?"

The question strangled her. A surge of adrenaline anchored her more firmly to the present, forcing a horrifying moment of clarity.

Because there was nothing there.

No answers to his questions.

She couldn't remember…. There was nothing, except for the gun pointing at her, and that final scream. A child's scream.

"Run!" She tried to sit up. She had to get out of there. "I have to go back, before—"

"Go back where?" He held her down until she stopped struggling.

She blindly felt for his hand.

He started at her touch, then squeezed her fingers. "There's nowhere to go right now. Let me take care of you, then we'll figure out the rest. It's going to be okay."

The sentiment sent her fighting again.

"You've taken quite a blow to your head." He restrained her as gently as before. "You need immediate surgery, but you're safe. You're not alone. I'm not going to let anything happen to you."

A mask was placed over her mouth and nose.

"Breathe normally." He nodded to someone behind her, then smiled again. "Let yourself fall asleep. I promise, I'll be here when you wake up. You can trust me."

She was in bad shape—she'd seen the truth in his eyes. In the barely controlled urgency behind the orders he'd issued. The right side of her head felt like it was on fire. The nightmare—it had been real. And now she could die. But worse, she'd...

Failed...

She'd failed at something important.... And now...

Someone she cared about deeply, someone she couldn't remember, was in danger.

Please, she begged him with her eyes.

Please, she'd begged someone else a long time ago. *Stay. Don't go away....*

"It will be okay," he promised. "Trust me."

And she did.

She shouldn't. That long-ago voice had promised the same thing, and lied. But the anesthesia was enticing her to let go. A cloud of security blanketed the fear.

She could finally stop running. From what, she had no idea. But just this once, she could stop running.

"FINISH PREPPING HER," Robert Livingston demanded, his gaze lowering to his patient's relaxed features. "I want to be in there looking for bleeders in five minutes."

He made himself let go of her hand as she was intubated. Then he turned to study the portable CT scans and focus on the challenges of the case. Anything but accepting the unprofessional protectiveness he'd felt for the gravely injured woman who'd been frantically trying to crawl off his operating table.

Jane Doe's skull hadn't been breached by whatever had struck her—a pipe, maybe something smaller. But there was significant damage. The CT scan showed a compound fracture, a subdural hematoma beneath and other lesions that could become life-threatening. Reversing the damage, even delicately, would increase the risk of complications. But he had to stop the bleeding and remove any debris that might cause a clot or escalating pressure and swelling.

Then all there'd be left to do was wait, and hope.

It will be okay....

Trust me.

Every person in the O.R. had frozen at his unprofessional lapse. Her odds of a full recovery were fifty-fifty at best. Her terror upon waking was understandable. The police had classified this a typical mugging, but hers was one of the worst robbery outcomes Robert had seen. And he'd seen plenty. Nothing might ever be *okay* for this patient again.

But when she'd grabbed his hand, he'd fallen into those expressive brown eyes—just like Jacob's eyes. And in the face of her all-consuming fear, he'd found himself promising whatever he had to, just as he had with his baby brother over twenty years ago.

"I have to rescrub." He turned away while his surgical intern stabilized the patient's head, covering everything but the shaved area around the injury with sterile dressings. "We open in two minutes."

It had been drilled into him in med school that his patients' problems outside the hospital were beyond his control. So were the many possible complications they faced during recovery. But in the O.R., the control was his. And he was good at what he did. The best neurosurgeon in Georgia, tops in his field nationally. He lost very few patients, and he wasn't losing this one.

He turned on the taps and lathered up. Breaking the seal on a brush, he scrubbed from his nails to his elbows. His fingers clenched at the memory of Jane Doe's hand trembling in his. There'd been strength in her. Determination to run, even though she'd been weak from heavy blood loss. He'd found himself equally determined to protect her. To defend her from whatever she was so certain was closing in.

The brush clattered to the floor.

Damn it!

He opened another from its sterile packaging.

Focus, man.

He was a doctor. His patient was perfectly safe now, and it was the police's job to keep her that way. He'd said what he had to. Calmed her down so his team could finish prepping for surgery. He'd have done the same thing for anyone in her emotional state. This case was no different than any other.

He scrubbed harder.

He'd never promised a patient anything before. And he'd have promised this one even more. Whatever it took to ease the panic consuming her.

You have to help me get out of here….

He shook his head and began to rinse—fingers up, letting the sterile water wash the soap downward.

It was time to work his magic, then send Jane Doe on her way. He'd patch her up, so she could go wherever she so desperately needed to go—and before he became even more irrationally attached to helping her get there.

TEN HOURS LATER at a quarter past four in the morning—exhausted, showered and chugging coffee to keep himself awake—Robert walked off Atlanta Memorial's central elevator onto the ICU floor. A half hour ago, an unconscious Jane Doe had been moved from recovery to an observation suite, right about the time Robert should have been dragging himself home to bed. He'd be on-call again in just six hours.

But he couldn't leave.

He'd checked with the supervising floor nurse. No one had materialized and asked to be notified about Jane Doe's condition. There was still no contact information on her chart, except for the names of the Atlanta Police Department officers who'd found her and called for the ambulance.

She was completely alone.

He turned into the dimly lit room that was little more than a glass-enclosed, corner cubicle with two doors that offered easy access from either hallway that ran past it. When Jane Doe was awake and downgraded to a less critical condition, blinds could be drawn to offer her privacy. Until then, she would be observed 24/7 by the top-notch nursing team that ran the floor like a fine-tuned machine.

She lay propped on a nest of starched, white pillows. Her shoulder-length, ebony hair spilled around her face and over the dressing that covered his work. He consulted her chart and tracked her vitals, then double-checked her heart rate and breathing with the stethoscope he was still wearing, even though he'd traded his scrubs for street clothes.

Officially, her condition was guarded, but stable. He'd done a hell of a job, delicately patching up the damage as noninvasively as possible. Still, there was no telling how long it would take before she woke, or what kind of complications might await them once she did.

The best post-op treatment for traumatic brain injury was rest and gentle stimulation. Having people who knew the patient spend time interacting with her, enticing her to reattach to the world around her.

Only his Jane Doe didn't have anyone to sit beside her and talk about home, or the family pet, or a child's crazy day at school.

His Jane Doe?

She didn't belong to him, or anyone else it would seem.

Robert studied the armed APD officers positioned in the hall. He wasn't the only one standing watch tonight. The police were impatient to question her as soon as she woke.

A little too impatient. So much for this being a typical mugging.

Taking another sip of his coffee, Robert set the cup down and sat in the lone chair beside the bed. He hesitated, then reached for her hand.

Her fingers felt so tiny in his, and not just because

he was a big man. She'd put up a hell of a fight when she'd come to. She'd been stronger than any of them had expected. But the hospital bed, the blankets and sheets, seemed to swallow her now. She was completely vulnerable.

As vulnerable as his baby brother, Jacob, had been, when he'd slowly slipped away, still clinging to Robert's hand.

Robert threaded his fingers through his patient's, feeling his professionalism evaporate as he remembered the promise he'd made her—a woman he knew nothing about, whom he had no business promising anything.

Except he had. The same promise he'd made his brother.

I'll be here when you wake up.

LEXI WAS GONE. But not for good.

She wouldn't forget about her.

She'd promised.

Evie clutched Felix closer and huddled deeper into the kitchen chair she'd been told not to move from. Her father shouted the f-bomb in the next room. Again. Something about the cop cars that had barreled into the alley while Evie was snatched away in one of her father's SUVs.

"...too damn close! How could you have been so stupid. What the hell were Alexa and my daughter doing there in the first place!"

Silence came next. Which meant Si and Am were

probably just standing there with their stupid mouths hanging open.

"Answer me!" her father demanded, his voice quieter.

Quiet was scarier than when he was shouting.

The mumbling that followed made her think of the bumbling, sneaky Siamese cats Evie had nicknamed her latest bodyguards after—the feline villains from her favorite Disney movie. She couldn't hear a word the two hulking men were saying. She'd been banished to snack on milk and cookies in the kitchen. She was fourteen, for goodness' sake, and she was hooked on kiddie food and kiddie movies.

A dream world, Lexi had called Evie's life. But today hadn't been a dream.

Lexi had made something up about leaving her PDA at the warehouse when she'd been there last week. She'd begged the Siamese think tank to drive her over to look for it. Evie had stowed away behind her seat in the SUV, under a blanket, like they'd been planning forever. Except they hadn't planned on everything being so last-minute. Or on Evie forgetting Felix when they ran, then being a baby about it. Or on someone at the condo realizing they were both nowhere to be found and sounding the alarm.

Who knew Si and Am had enough brains to put two and two together?

Everything had gone way wrong. She and Lexi hadn't made it out, and—

"You better hope to God she's not dead!" Her father's threat made Evie jump.

Her hand knocked over the milk he'd poured her before he'd headed into the study to grill his men, telling her not to budge while he was gone.

Lexi wasn't dead. She wasn't gone for good. She was coming back. She wouldn't forget Evie.

She'd promised.

Evie held fast to Felix and inched toward the kitchen's ultramodern center island, glancing at the door as she passed. The island was made of smooth, cold metal, just like everything else in the room. Everything in the condo felt colder, now that Lexi was gone.

Evie grabbed the black kitchen towel that matched the dishes her mother never would have let her father buy…back before her mother had gone away, too. She mopped up her mess, her attention shifting between what she was doing and the phone on the wall near the refrigerator.

What was she more afraid of—her father, or not following Lexi's instructions?

Don't be stupid, Evie told herself. But she inched closer to the phone anyway. *He'll be really mad if he catches you.*

Mad?

Her father never got *just* mad.

His temper would keep building. He was just warming up with his men. He'd be back for her sooner or later, no matter what Evie did.

She wasn't allowed to use the phone—ever. She was barely allowed to breathe, unless she cleared it with him first. She definitely wasn't allowed to try to run away, but she had. She'd begged Lexi, and they'd planned it and waited, and then she'd messed it all up.

And now she was the one her father was really mad at, not the Siamese. Mad like she hadn't seen him since the night he'd caught her mom packing her and Evie's things. The night her mom had gone away and never come back.

What difference did it make if Evie used the phone now?

She reached for the portable while her memory fumbled for numbers. The numbers Lexi had helped her memorize. *Just in case,* Lexi had said. In case of what, they'd never talked about.

A series of crashes, what sounded like a fist hitting flesh and a large body—Si or Am?—destroying furniture as it fell, brought the numbers back in a rush.

She had to reach Lexi.

Everything's going to be okay. I won't let him hurt you again. I'll never leave you here....

Dialing was hard. Evie's heart and her arm and every other part of her body kept jerking, telling her to run, even though running never did anything but make what came next worse.

Her mother was gone.

Lexi was gone....

No! Lexi would be back.

A computer voice came on the line. Evie was instructed to leave a message. To take the biggest risk of her life.

She couldn't breathe.

Talk, you big baby!

Get her back here.

So what if it was going to hurt again for a little while? It was worth it. Lexi would come back. She'd make the hurt stop for good.

"Um…" She peeked over her shoulder. *No names.* Lexi had said no real names. *You never know who'll be listening.* "This is…Bambi. I…I'm looking for Thumper. I need…I need to talk to her. I need…Felix and I need to—"

The phone struck the side of her head as it was yanked away, booped off and thrown across the room.

"What the hell do you think you're doing!" her father whispered in her face.

He shook her, both hands clenched on her shoulders. Hard. Harder! She could already feel the blow to come.

His arm reared back, his hand ready to fly. Evie cringed, then thought of her mother, always shrinking away, and Lexi, fighting back against Si in the alley behind the warehouse. Lexi's fear had changed to something dark and fierce when Evie was dragged, screaming, into her father's SUV. Something like *take your best shot, you bastard.* Something brave that Evie wanted for herself.

She lifted her chin and glared up at the man she'd

been terrified of every day for fourteen years. He'd taken her mother away. His men had hurt Lexi and left her for dead. Evie clutched Felix closer—her only friend before Lexi came. The last thing her mother had given her.

And in her mind, she was suddenly the baby ant staring up at the scary, brainless grasshopper that was about to strike.

Man, would you knock off the Disney!

But that's how it felt. Like she was dead meat, only she was done being scared and bullied and afraid. From now on, she was going to be like Lexi.

No matter where he takes you, I'll find you, sweetheart, Lexi had promised. *Even if I have to leave, I won't forget you. I'll come back for you. Be brave, and when you can, call the number I gave you.*

Be brave…

"Tell me what happened in the alley." Her father shook her again, one hand still raised, his lips twisted into a threatening smile. "If Lexi's dead, it's all your fault. Tell me what happened."

Evie didn't answer. She wasn't telling him anything. And Lexi wasn't dead.

His arm dropped. He pulled her into a gentle hug. The smell of his aftershave made her stomach churn. Made the Bambi weakness come back, the kind that had left the little fawn cowering in a thicket thinking he'd never be safe again.

"Don't make me punish you, my darling," her father crooned. "You know I don't want to punish you. Give Daddy what he needs. Be a good girl. Tell me why you and Lexi were running away. Tell me where she was going."

He'd punish her no matter what she said, because that was the part he liked best. That and the way he always got what he wanted in the end. In the end, she was always Daddy's good little girl.

She'd been safe from it for a while. Lexi had protected her. Now it was Evie's turn to do the protecting and to hang on until Lexi came back. Whatever it took.

She turned her head and kissed her father's cheek, swallowing the reflex to puke when he chuckled and patted her back.

"Good girl." He smiled down, his eyes soft, relaxed. So sure he had her. "Now tell Daddy everything."

She ran her fingers up the buttons of his dress shirt, brushing across his pounding heart.

Pervert.

Then she smiled her little-girl smile, the one Daddy liked best. Braced herself without moving a muscle. Thought of Lexi and tried to believe she really could be brave, too.

She hugged Felix closer and took a deep breath.

"No," she said sweetly, pasting her smile in place and watching her father's rage roar back.

CHAPTER TWO

RUN! SHE SCREAMED IN the nightmare. *It's going to be okay. I promise. But we have to move.*

"It's going to be okay," echoed a voice beside her. "Can you try opening your eyes?"

The voice was too warm to be part of the nightmare, not right.

Something wasn't right.

Open your eyes! Run!

A gunshot shattered the darkness. A child's scream. So much pain. She squeezed the hand she found holding hers.

She wasn't alone.

It's going to be okay.

She jerked away. She had to get to the street.... Had to get her out... Keep fighting... But she couldn't...couldn't move.

She'd failed....

Failure's only a place to start, her mind heckled in a feminine voice that wasn't her own. Annoying and chipper, the long-ago voice clashed with her nightmare, too. Her pain. *It's only the end if you quit trying....*

And so she'd keep trying, whether she wanted to or not.

"IT'S OKAY," Robert assured his waking patient. Relief flooded him despite her agitation. He pressed the call button for the nurse. "Relax. You're safe. It's safe here."

"Bambi." She struggled against his grip, her eyes still closed. "Have to go back... The apartment... Get to the apartment..."

Bambi?

He smiled at that. Definitely not what he'd expected to come out of her mouth next, though he'd heard crazier from patients over the years.

She pulled away with a burst of strength. Then she slapped the tubing that fed oxygen into her nostrils.

He guided her arm back to the bed and reset the tubing's prongs. "Open your eyes for me. Time to wake up."

The sooner, the better for her recovery.

For his peace of mind.

No longer fighting, she scowled. Her head lolled away from his touch, her expression more animated by the second.

Good.

He wanted to smooth away the wrinkles lining her forehead.

Bad.

His job was to get her conscious, no matter what was haunting her. Period. Actually, waking her was the ICU recovery team's job. He was going to catch hell when word got around that he'd been lurking at a patient's side since surgery.

"Wake up and tell me about Bambi," he urged.

Movement at the door caught his eye.

"Bambi, huh?" The tall, curvy blonde's chuckle was an easy and light sound that made her the star of the pediatric floor. "That's a tactic I haven't heard a doctor use before."

Hell had caught up with him.

Kate Rhodes was mouthy and sweet, and as loyal a woman as Robert had ever met. An ace at her job. A true patient's advocate.

"Jane Doe's talking in her sleep." He turned his back to the smirking nurse who for five years had been his wife.

"And you were talking back, for the second off-shift this weekend?" Kate stepped to the foot of the bed, her eyes scanning the various monitors and displays tracking the mystery woman's vitals. "The entire hospital is laying bets on whether or not you've finally cracked. I've assured everyone that isn't possible. But I figured I'd better do a bit of recon to protect my stake."

"I'm trying to help her. She's a patient…."

"Who has a round-the-clock staff of expertly trained nurses looking out for her."

"Have to get back…" Jane murmured, tugging against his grasp. "Have to get her out…"

Kate's gaze shifted to Robert's hand grasping Jane's.

"Just a patient?" She and her quirked eyebrow clearly hadn't been born yesterday.

"She's…" He looked past Kate to the APD watchdogs in the hall. They were champing at the bit, more anxious to talk to their witness by the hour. "She seems to be in a lot of trouble, and—"

"And beyond monitoring the coma she's flirting with, you think you can do *what* to help her exactly?"

Kate herself had not too long ago been the poster child for overidentifying with her patients and tossing professional boundaries out the window. Which made her field trip to ICU and pseudo-lecture even more annoying.

Robert rubbed his thumb over Jane's unbelievably soft wrist. "I can't help her with whatever those officers are waiting to talk to her about, but I can make sure she's stable before they get in here."

"Which you've done, by repairing the damage to her skull. Why all the handholding?"

"She's had no visitors," he reasoned. "And frequent verbal stimulation can be key in cases like this."

Kate's attention strayed to his touch on Jane's arm. "Or maybe it's got something to do with her being vulnerable and needing someone to save her?"

"Kate—" Robert buried both hands in the pockets of his scrubs "—don't start."

"I've known this was a thing for you." Kate always had been tenacious, when she was working her way around a point she refused to budge from. "I get that our marital problems had more to do with your guilt over losing Jacob than they did you and me."

"Kate—"

"You always had to be sure I was okay. And you couldn't handle that I was never going to be okay back then. We'd never have made it work, and it was as much my fault as yours. But now you're letting the past mess with what you've built here at Atlanta Memorial."

"I'm her doctor, Kate."

"You're her surgeon, Robert. You saved her life. Job well done. But with any other patient, you'd have moved on days ago. Sprinted, actually. You're the Lone Ranger of neurosurgery, always riding off into the sunset to save another day. Never enough time to eat or sleep or build real relationships. No distractions allowed—until now."

"I'm not distracted." He checked his watch. He had a whole hour before his next on-call shift. Another hour beyond that, he'd be prepping for surgery.

"Right. Except for—"

"No!" Jane lurched forward, panting, her eyes open but blind. Her fingers shook, yanking at the cables and leads hooking her to a sea of diagnostic equipment. "Get to the street... Have to get to the street! Leave Felix... I'll come back for him later..."

Kate helped him ease Jane back to her pillows.

"She's waking?" Lieutenant Downing asked from the doorway. He was the one officer who'd been there around the clock, while the other uniforms rotated in shifts. "I need to speak with her as soon—"

"As soon as she's making any sense, you'll get your chance," Robert asserted. "Until then, get out."

"No!" Jane kept struggling, her words slurred. "Have to…if something happens… Call me… remember…Thumper. I won't let him hurt you again…."

"It's okay," Robert whispered down at her. "I said get out!" he snarled over his shoulder. "What?"

The question was for his ex and yet another of her raised eyebrows.

"How's that not-distracted thing working out for you?" she asked.

"Isn't your job a couple of floors away?" Kate might be right, but she didn't have to be so damn smug about it.

Jane's grip tightened. She blinked up at him, her vulnerable gaze sharpening more by the second while she took in her surroundings.

"Who are you!" she whimpered, the fight gone out of her. "Where… Where am I?"

"I'll send a nurse in," Kate said as she backed off. "But if you don't mind, I'll keep an eye on things up here for a while. Looks like I won't be the only one."

An ICU nurse and the chief of staff made their way into the room. Kate's professional nod toward both Seth Washington and the still-hovering Lieutenant Downing held no hint of the personal things she and Robert had discussed.

She was a good friend. She'd cover Robert's ass, no matter how far off the reservation she clearly thought he'd gone.

"Don't try and figure everything out at once," said the angel standing over her.

An angel dressed in soft blue, who'd been with her before…promising her…something…

His was the voice that kept breaking through the darkness. He kept telling her it was safe to wake up. The kind of safety that evaporated every time the nightmare returned.

How long had she been asleep?

Where… Where was she?

She glanced around the room.

A hospital room…

She's a patient….

I'll send a nurse in….

Overhead lights sliced into her eyes. She winced, clenching the blanket beneath her fingers. The men hovering just inside the doorway came into focus. Tall men. One wearing a suit, the other some kind of uniform.

"I…" she croaked. "I thought…"

Nothing…

Every thought was gone. Nothing would stick.

Her gaze swung back to her angel. His golf shirt.
Faded jeans.

"I'm in a hospital?"

"You have a severe head injury." His hand circled
her wrist while he studied his watch. Taking her
pulse. A doctor, not an angel. "And you—"

"Is she awake enough to talk?" The other man's
voice was deeper, more determined. Even a little
desperate.

He stepped to the bed, his hands loosely clasped
behind his back, his legs braced apart.

That's when his uniform registered.

A cop, not a doctor.

Her heart gave a panicky hiccup, even though she
didn't recognize him any more than she did the others.

"Two days recovering from neurological trauma?" The compassion in the doctor's voice washed
over her. His thumb stroked her wrist. "I don't think
so. And I can't make an accurate read of her condition while you're scaring her to death. Please wait in
the hallway, Lieutenant."

"The man's just doing his job, Robert," the other
man said.

He, too, stepped closer. Him and his expensive
suit.

The man in charge.

"I need to know if she remembers anything about
the circumstances around the shooting." The officer
was calmer now, but still staring too hard and
standing too close.

The shooting?

What had been tiny blips—electronic pinpricks of background noise—pinged faster. She couldn't breathe over the pounding in her head. She closed her eyes against the rush. But it didn't help.

Nothing could, not even her doctor's soothing, "It's going to be all right," which he immediately followed with a cold, "Get out!" aimed at the others.

How could it be all right, when the thing terrifying her wasn't her head injury—received during a shooting!—but the rest…?

The instinct to run from the cop… Being certain she was in danger the second she saw him. That she had to get away…

But away from what?

What had she gotten herself into? Who…

Who she was?

Oh, my God!

"I…" She clung to the doctor's hand, desperate for the security his touch gave her, even though she knew it wasn't real. "I can't remember…anything…."

CHAPTER THREE

"SHE HAS AMNESIA!" Lieutenant Downing's voice was rough with disbelief.

Robert ignored him. "I need this room cleared." Robert tried to ease Jane back to the bed. "Rest for a few minutes until we know more about your condition."

"I can't..." She resisted the gentle pressure of his hands, struggling to sit up. "I don't know... Who am I?"

Robert had absolutely no idea how to respond.

Her shaky gaze shifted to her APD watchdog.

"What..." She lifted a hand to her throat. "What's going on?"

"We were kind of hoping you could shed some light on that." Downing's smile was grim. "I was in one of two patrol cars that arrived on the scene where you were struggling with several men. Shots were fired. Your attackers piled into a vehicle and sped away. I checked your condition and radioed for an ambulance, then waited with you while the other car pursued the black SUV. But whoever did this to you evaded capture. Their plates matched a twenty-year-old piece of junk that was stolen over a month ago. The trail ends there, I'm afraid."

"How much do you remember?" Robert checked her pupil reflexes while he sifted through the details Downing had shared. Jane Doe was lucky to be alive. "Tell me the last thing you remember."

"I…" She swallowed, shaking with the effort. Her hand dropped to the mattress. He covered it with his own. Curling his fingers around hers was becoming a habit. "I remember waking up. You were there…." She turned her head toward him, winced and closed her eyes. "There's…a gunshot, maybe. A scream… Nothing… Nothing else. It's… nothing's clear."

"The SUV shot its way out of the scene," Downing offered. "Do you remember anything about why they were after you? What—"

"No!" Jane clung to Robert. Her eyes closed. "Nothing. I can't remember…anything. Except…"

Her body jerked.

"Oh, God!" She buried her head against Robert's chest, her body going limp.

He slid her gently back to the bed.

"Out!" he said to Downing.

He double-checked the monitors. No indications of anything but loss of consciousness.

Jane's head began shaking from side to side again. Her hand clenched in his, then clenched harder.

"Run!" Her eyes jerked open. "Oh, my God!"

"What are you remembering?" Downing stepped closer.

"I said get out!" Robert braced a hand on the officer's chest, as if he could hold off a man who outweighed him by at least fifty solidly packed pounds.

"Dr. Livingston!" Seth, one of Robert's oldest friends, brushed Robert's grip away from the scowling policeman. "Focus on your patient. Lieutenant Downing, I'll speak with you in the hallway."

Seth ushered the lieutenant out.

"I have to…" Jane struggled to sit again, wobbled and would have wilted back to the pillow, except Robert caught her. She grabbed the front of his shirt. "I have to go back. Get her out…"

"You got out. You're safe. Now let me help you."

"Where am I?" Jane's eyes scanned the ICU cubicle, crazed. She was like a wounded animal, too weak to flee. "Who… Why can't I remember who—"

"Don't try." He checked her pupils again. Reminded himself that confusion and disorientation were just as common with head trauma as temporary amnesia. "Can you squeeze my fingers?"

"What?"

He placed the first two fingers of both his hands within the circle of hers. He had to stay focused on his job, nothing more. *Calm down, so you can calm the patient down.* "Squeeze for me."

Her chest rose and fell.

Shock. She was in shock and scared to death. Perfectly understandable. He'd be more concerned if she wasn't. She clearly remembered nothing more than the disjointed ramblings she'd uttered over the last forty-eight hours. From the sound of it, she could recall very little about being hurt or her life before the assault. Of course she was scared.

"I…" She blinked. "You… I know you…."

He weathered his own jolt of recognition—the certainty that he somehow knew her, too. Really *knew* this stranger.

"I'm Dr. Robert Livingston. Your surgeon."

"Surgeon?" Her hand lifted to the injured area above her left ear. "What…"

"It's often difficult to remember things for a while after a head injury, just—"

"Head injury?" Her fingers stilled over the bandage dressing her wound. "What—"

"Squeeze first one, then the other?" He pulled her hand away and inserted his fingers into her grasp again, smiling in approval while she squeezed in sequence. "Again, this time the left one first."

He nodded as she complied, hating her confusion but ignoring the urge to let her rest. He needed to complete at least a preliminary examination. When she succeeded, he smiled again.

"Now, can you look at the nurse for me?" He waited until she did, relaxing more with each response. "Good. Now squeeze my fingers. Do you remember which one you squeezed first last time?"

She looked back.

"Keep your eyes on the nurse." When she did, he added, "Squeeze my fingers in the same sequence as before, while you read her name badge for me."

Jane's left hand squeezed, then the right, her grip stronger.

"Nurse Beckham," she said.

"Very good." Satisfied, he motioned for the sedative to be administered through her IV. "Now, follow the tip of my pen with your eyes only."

Confused eyes followed his pen until it moved in front of his face. Then her gaze blurred with tears, trashing the last of his professionalism.

"You're safe now," he assured her. "You're going to be okay."

She shook her head, then winced at what must have been a killer headache.

"I—I can't remember anything." Her next blink was slower, the next even slower. Her lids fluttered back open and held. "I…there's something…"

"It can wait," he insisted.

Deirdre Beckham fiddled with the valve dripping a saline solution, a broad-spectrum antibiotic, pain medication and the mild relaxant he'd prescribed into the tube in Jane's arm.

"Rest is the best thing for you," he said.

Screw the APD and whatever they thought they could get out of this woman. Screw leaving Jane now, when it was becoming more obvious by the second that the danger to her went far beyond the damage he'd repaired in the O.R.

Her hold on his hand fumbled, her head shaking.

"Was there a police officer here?" Her eyes squinted. "Was...was I...I heard a gunshot?"

"Let it go," Robert insisted.

Damn Downing for pushing her.

"Doctor." Deirdre motioned to the cardiac monitor.

Jane's heart rate was spiking, despite the sedative.

"Fighting the meds will only slow your recovery and the return of your memory," he explained. "Your mind will tell you what you need to know when it's time. Don't force it. Just rest. You're safe here."

"You don't understand." Her heavy lids stayed closed. "I don't know why, but...I think...rememberingis..." Her words faded into a continuous slur. "Feelsl ikeam atterof life ordeath..."

The drugs took her under. Her pulse finally settled, while Robert's heart was trying to throb its way out of his chest.

He glanced to where Seth was handling the APD in the hallway. He looked back at the woman still clutching his fingers like she'd never let go of them. His *patient*. Only Jane was less of a patient each time she reached for him. She'd touched him deeper in just a few days than any woman ever had. And now she couldn't remember anything but him and the fact that she was in grave danger.

Medically, she was improving better than could be expected. He was needed elsewhere, by other patients. And Seth's glower from the hallway made it clear Robert's unprecedented hovering had already caused more than enough trouble for the hospital's administration.

It was time to get a grip and focus on what he did best. As Kate had helpfully pointed out, it was time to move on to the next person who needed him.

Except shutting down his emotions and simply doing the job wasn't working this time.

Not with Jane.

"DR. WASHINGTON, if we don't get the information we need from the patient soon," Lieutenant Downing insisted, "we'll lose whatever chance we have to track her attackers. The window for finding someone who's committed a random street crime is forty-eight hours, and we're already beyond that."

Seth Washington took inventory of the two officers still flanking their mystery patient's door. And then there was the lieutenant. APD had permanently stationed themselves within spitting distance of Jane Doe.

"What kind of information, exactly, are you gunning for?" he asked, shifting his attention to inside the ICU observation room.

Robert had calmed the young woman enough to examine her. She seemed to be resting now. Which should have meant Seth's job there was done. Except one of his best doctors—his best friend—had nearly come to blows with Downing.

"We're looking for whatever she can tell us," Downing persisted. "We need to know more about the people responsible for hurting her."

"People?" Seth's attention snapped back to the officer. There had been genuine emotion in Downing's voice, but the man had already yanked his professional mask back in place. "I thought she was mugged."

Downing's slow blink was too practiced a non-response.

"Exactly what sort of *people* do you suspect?" Seth asked. "You said this was a random street crime."

"APD procedure is to rule nothing out, until we have more evidence to go on."

"I'm the chief of staff of the largest hospital in the southeast, Lieutenant. My E.R. treats over a dozen mugging victims a night. If your department committed this many resources to every assault case, you'd never get anything else done. So I have to assume there's something about this particular victim that your superiors haven't seen fit to share with me."

"Details of an ongoing investigation are released on a need-to-know basis." The clipped efficiency of Downing's latest story suited the officer.

It just didn't suit Seth's overtaxed patience.

"I'm where the buck stops around here, Lieutenant. Which pretty much means I need to know everything *you* know about any danger a patient and the staff I assign to work with her are in."

"Who said she's still in danger?"

Seth waited in silence, not feeling obliged to state the obvious. Robert approached from behind them.

"I'll have to discuss the matter with my supervisors before releasing any information," Downing finally said. "APD isn't the only agency interested in this case, and at the moment I'm not completely certain who I'm taking my orders from."

"Have whatever discussions you need to." Seth absorbed the fact that the officer didn't sound any happier with the situation than he was. "Until her surgeon's cleared her for questioning, I'll be limiting access to Jane Doe to essential medical personnel only."

Downing's gaze flicked between Seth and Robert, then the big man headed for the elevator, his cell phone already at his ear.

The officers flanking the patient's room stayed put.

"What was that about?" Robert asked.

Seth confirmed that Jane Doe was asleep, then he headed for the stairs. Maybe jogging the flight up to his office would clear his head.

"Make sure a nurse is monitoring the woman at all times," he said over his shoulder, "then get your butt up to my office. Once I've arranged for someone to cover your surgeries, I'll tell you what *that* was all about. And then you can tell me why I'm not going to regret buying you extra time, before whoever the cops are fronting for shows up to interview your patient."

"DOES THAT MEAN you're encouraged by her post-op progress?" Robert's chief asked an hour later. Seth sat in his ultrasoft executive chair, his feet kicked up on his desk. "Because if she's out of immediate danger, I don't see the harm in—"

"I've only managed a few basic tests to set a baseline," Robert hedged. It wasn't exactly the truth, and his friend would know that. But Seth seemed equally suspicious of the rotating band of cops lurking about the ICU. "Her memory is still impaired, and her anxiety shoots through the roof every time Lieutenant Downing opens his mouth. I need to observe her in a controlled setting, before I can upgrade her post-op status and move her to a recovery floor. Until then, the police should back off."

"Upgrading her condition is your call." Seth settled deeper into his chair, in that absent way that meant he was talking more to himself than anyone else. "But it's looking like APD or someone else might want a hand in deciding the rest."

"The rest of what?" Robert picked up a stress ball that was a big, yellow smiley face and began squeezing the hell out of the perky thing. When Seth's only response was to rub the back of one index finger under his jaw and stare at the meticulously organized clutter covering his desk, Robert tossed the foam toy at his friend's head.

Seth snagged "Smiley" without looking up, then tossed it back before plucking a sheet of paper from the top of the stack nearest his elbow. He offered it— an e-mail printout—to Robert.

The APD chief of police was requesting that his

officers be given immediate access to the unidentified victim as soon as she regained consciousness, and that Jane Doe remain in the more easily secured ICU until further notice. There was to be no official record of her being admitted to the hospital. Any attempted contact from anyone besides APD was to be reported to Lieutenant Downing immediately.

Their patient was not only a Jane Doe. Outside the four walls of her ICU cubicle, she evidently didn't exist.

Robert had his chief's full attention when he looked up.

"I doubt whoever needs the answers Downing's dredging for," Seth said, "is going to be content to wait while you hold your patient's hand."

"She panicked. I had to sedate her."

"She panicked because she couldn't remember anything. Not an uncommon short-term result of traumatic brain injury and surgery. What *is* uncommon is my head neurosurgeon bullying a cop in a display of overprotectiveness that ended with him medicating a patient, rather than letting his staff stabilize her."

Robert squirmed in his chair.

"I did what was necessary to get Lieutenant Downing out of the room."

"Yes." The lines bracketing Seth's frown deepened. "But the information Downing is here to retrieve seems to have a limited shelf life. If that e-mail is any indication, he'll be back. As Jane Doe's *doctor,* wouldn't it make more sense to be helping her remember whatever she can, so the authorities can protect her and then leave her in peace?"

Seth had been Robert's mentor. The best man at Robert's wedding. The only ear Robert had trusted ranting into when things with Kate broke to the point that there was no fixing them. They knew each other's skeletons, or at least enough of them to provide the unspoken support they'd each needed over the years, while they maintained the ruthless emotional control their jobs required.

"She's in trouble." Robert walked to the picture window that offered a panoramic view of Atlanta's majestic skyline. Forward-thinking architecture had converged over the decades with old-world charm, all built on the ruins of what the South's graceful grand dame had been before the destruction of the Civil War. "Jane's a survivor, but she's nowhere near strong enough yet to fight for herself."

"Jane?" Seth's expression clouded with concern. "I've seen her chart. You outdid yourself with her surgery. Now that she's regained consciousness so swiftly, it'll be difficult to convince anyone she's too fragile to interview."

"Hold them off." Robert flipped back his lab coat and planted his hands on his hips. "Say whatever you have to. She needs more time."

"She needs more time?" Seth fingered the gold-plated letter opener that had been a final Christmas gift from his soon-to-be ex-wife.

"Okay, *I* need more time." Not to mention a full night's sleep. Except every time Robert closed his eyes, he saw the fear in Jane's gaze, her vulnerability while she grappled with the impulse to get back to someone or something she couldn't remember— to get away from someone he suspected might be the very men stationed outside her door. "There's more going on than the authorities are saying. More than memory loss about a mugging. The patient's improving remarkably, considering her injuries, but she's in danger, and—"

"And when a mugging victim's in danger, naturally the last thing you want to see in her doorway is a swarm of local police trying to protect her."

"Is that what they're there for? Two beat cops and a lieutenant seems overkill for a random crime. Looks more like a fishing expedition, with my patient as bait."

Seth braced his forearms on the desk and sat forward.

"And you're basing this assumption on what?"

"It's just…a feeling."

"A feeling?"

"I promised her…" Robert finally admitted. "She was terrified and on my table. Slipping in and out of nightmares or memories or God knows what. She reached for my hand, and before I could stop myself…I promised her everything would be okay."

"You promised her." Seth's right eye seemed to be twitching, though it could have been the play of morning light and shadow coming off the blinds. "Your patient had a critical brain injury, she's the focus of an APD violent crime investigation, and you promised her everything's going to be okay?"

Yeah. Seth's right eye was definitely twitching, along with the fingers he was drumming against the ink blotter beneath the letter opener.

"I can't explain it." Robert shrugged. "Except that—"

"You've lost your mind?"

"I think her medical condition is the least of her problems and—"

"You've lost your mind?"

"And she seems to have no one else. No one's asked about her, except the authorities, who only want whatever information is locked inside her memory."

And he wanted to be what she needed for just a little longer. To just be with her.

Maybe he *had* lost his mind.

"I'm assuming you have a plan?" Seth said. "You always do."

"We keep the authorities away long enough for her to figure things out. You have the power to overrule my orders, but—"

"Now why would I do that?" His friend stood, clipping his BlackBerry to his belt. "Watching you come unglued over a patient is more intriguing than watching Kate fall for that bulldog of an attorney she married. You two are better than a soap opera."

"I'm not coming unglued—" Robert followed his boss out of the office. "I'm—"

"You're hopeless. Forty-eight hours since you set eyes on the woman, and you've barely left her side. I'm canceling all but your most critical procedures, and you'll still be on-call if something juicy comes through the E.R. But until further notice, do what you can for your patient. I'll hold APD off. I'll run interference. But, Robert..."

Seth grabbed his arm before they reached the elevator that would take them back to ICU.

"Sometime soon, you're going to have to let her go."

"I know," Robert said.

The dread rushing through him at the thought was a foreign thing. Not something he'd ever wanted in his life. Since losing Jacob, first his education and then his work had consumed his life so completely, he'd easily kept emotional entanglements at a controlled distance, even during his marriage.

Until now.

CHAPTER FOUR

"LEXI. CAN YOU HEAR ME?"

She jerked toward consciousness. The voice was familiar, but not.

"Lexi?" it persisted.

Insistent.

Too close.

Lexi! her nightmare screamed.

A shadow moved from behind her. Before she could fire, the side of her head exploded.

"No!"

She couldn't open her eyes. Couldn't move, but she fought anyway.

Hard hands held her down. A man's hands.

Not her angel's.

"Shhh," he whispered close to her ear. "Stop fighting me. Let me help you. It's Rick. You have to—"

"Move!" *We have to move.... Forget about Felix.... Get to the street.* "Run!"

But she couldn't.

She'd failed.

Again.

Failure's only a place to start...

"Help us!" she cried.

She broke free of the jumble of voices and woke to find concerned brown eyes staring down at her. "Get away from me!" She shrank into the pillows.

The man let go, but he stayed beside the bed.

It was the police officer the doctor had thrown out before.

"You're..." She took in the empty room. "You're the—the lieutenant."

He waited for her to say more.

Was there more?

"I'm here to protect you," he said carefully. "Do you remember me?"

"I..." *Don't do this, Lexi! I'll do my best to protect you, but...* "I..."

New memories washed through her, leaving again before they made any sense. Voices with no faces. The lieutenant's voice, yes. His and too many others, swirling in threatening waves.

"Lexi?" He cupped her shoulder. "Are you—"

"Get away from me!"

She pushed, fought against his hold and rolled to the other side of the bed. Throwing aside the blanket, she tried to stand, her legs buckling, bells ringing in her throbbing head. She grabbed the bed rail for support, but fumbled and lost her grip.

He skirted around the bed, caught her close, a split second before she'd have hit the floor.

"Stop it," she begged.

Get to the street.

Run!

The nightmare stole what was left of her breath. The officer lifted her easily and settled her on the bed.

"I'm here to protect you." He eased back, but caught her again before she could move away. "Stop it, damn it, and I'll let you go!"

She did, the timbre of his voice shivering through her panic, sounding more familiar by the second. Just like his eyes—they were a shade of brown she could have sworn she'd seen before.

She shook her head.

He raised his palms before him, a nonthreatening gesture. "What are you remembering, Lexi?"

"Don't call me that!"

He eased another inch away. "You really don't remember, do you?"

"Remember what?"

I'm here to protect you....

"That—"

"What the hell do you think you're doing!" demanded a voice she did remember.

Her doctor. The angel from her dreams. Reality. All swirling together.

"Make it stop." She cradled her skull, jostling the dressing at her temple. She winced at the bite of pain.

"Take it easy." Her doctor brushed her hands away, then gently checked under the bandage. He circled her wrist in a loose grip to take her pulse. He was so calm. So safe. His touch washed through her anxiety, better than whatever meds were seeping through her IV.

Robert, he'd said his name was.

"Dr. Robert Livingston," she said out loud.

"Yes." Warmth radiated from his smile. Comfort. "You're remembering more each time you wake."

But the memories were worse than the nightmares.

"He…" She pointed at the officer. "I—"

"Look this way." The light Robert shined into her eyes blasted pain through her. "I'm sorry. Let me check the other pupil, then Lieutenant Downing and I will discuss whatever's on his mind. Everything's okay. Just relax for me."

His promise, her immediate acceptance of it, buffered the next blast of light.

"Good," he assured her. "Now try to rest."

He walked to the door, and waited silently for the other man to precede him.

"Sleep," he said. "I'll come back when I can."

Leaving her one last smile, he shut the door behind him.

She took stock of the room. Herself. Her heart, which was thundering harder than her head.

But what was scaring her most? That she didn't know who she was and how she'd gotten there, or why Lieutenant Downing thought she knew him? Or that the man who should be a total stranger, her doctor, possessed the touch she needed to calm the mixed up jumble her brain had become?

LETTING JANE DOE go was the last thing on Robert's mind as he faced Downing outside her room. Downing appeared equally disinclined to back off.

Big surprise.

"I have complete authority to be in that room," the lieutenant insisted. "In there, or anywhere else in this hospital. Don't think you can block me by drugging her or ordering me around. Just because you're—"

"I'm not *just* anything, Officer, I'm—"

"That's Lieutenant. I'm the senior APD officer on site, and your patient's protection detail is under my control. Her safety is my chief concern."

"Then I suggest you start by controlling yourself, *Lieutenant.*" Robert reined in the unreasonable urge to grab the larger man by his uniform shirt and shake him. "I'm not *just* that woman's doctor. I'm the head of neurology and a leading expert in brain injuries. You either back off and let her recover whatever memory she can when her brain's ready, or the information you're so determined to get may never be remembered. How are you going to find the criminals who put her in this condition if that happens?"

"I'm not the bully you're making me out to be." The tremor in Downing's voice almost had Robert believing him. "That woman's not just another statistic I need to write in a report so I can get home for dinner. I'm the one who brought her in. I saw what those bastards did to her. I'm trying to help—the only way I can."

Trying to help.

The same reasoning Robert had given Kate.

He took closer stock of the good officer. *Good* ringing true for the first time. There was something half-crazed in Downing's expression, something almost...

Personal.

"What's going on, Lieutenant Downing?" Robert had never been more certain that there was more to Jane's case than the cop was owning up to. "You've been prowling the hallway since she got out of surgery, and you've had men posted outside this door, and had the door on the other hallway locked, for two days. I warn you off—my boss does, too. But four hours later, here you are, pressuring her again."

"I'm doing my job." Downing was good, Robert would give him that. His bland expression was textbook badass. "What exactly is *your* interest, Dr. Livingston? The head of a surgical department, hovering for days by my witness's bedside. How do you manage that, exactly?"

"I thought she was a victim." Robert's fear for Jane kicked even higher. "Now she's a witness?"

Downing blinked. "You're evading my question."

"I'm informing you of hospital policy. Again." Their conversation was over. "Only immediate family and hospital staff are allowed in an ICU patient's room, regardless of how many e-mails your boss sends mine. You and your men are to remain in the hallway until my patient is stable and conscious for more than a few minutes at a time. I'll let you know when I'm satisfied she's ready to be interviewed."

The same hint of emotion Robert had seen before worked its way through Downing's professional mask—protectiveness.

Hurt her, and I'll kill you protectiveness.

"I'll be close by." Downing marched toward the elevators, punching away on his cell again and lifting it to his ear.

"I just bet you will be," Robert said after him.

He gazed through the windows into Jane's room, at a total loss for what to do next. After three hours of sifting paperwork and calling in markers, then throwing his weight around to secure enough surgeons to cover his overload of surgical cases, he was finally free to focus exclusively on Jane. Except he couldn't walk back into her room.

Downing might be overzealous, but he was genuinely concerned about his *witness*. But witness to what? Her own assault? Or was there something more?

Something the officer had stopped short of revealing.

It was starting to feel as if Jane had every reason to still be terrified of everything and everyone around her. Everyone but Robert. And each time Robert got near her, he lost another shred of his legendary objectivity. He wasn't going back into her room until her well-being was his only priority. He had to stop needing to feel the smoothness of her hand in his, the trust and acceptance rolling off of her, when she clung to him.

Jane needed her doctor's help, until she got her memory back. Nothing more. Then she'd need whatever protection Downing and his fellow officers could give her. Before too long, she'd be strong enough to rely on herself, and she wouldn't need any of them.

A fun fact Robert couldn't afford to forget.

THE NEXT TIME she woke, she was alone.

Her doctor was right. It was getting easier to think clearly. To remember more and more snatches of what had happened the last time. Things like the lieutenant pressing her for information. And feeling safe because…because Robert had swooped in to protect her.

Robert…

You'll know when he's right, the long-ago voice said. *You'll know it every time he touches you.*

She'd decided the voice that gave advice must belong to her mother—only a mother could manage to sound soothing and bossy at the same time. She closed her eyes. Saw Robert's warm, concerned eyes and a smile that felt real and right, and decided that maybe the mother voice wasn't so bad after all.

Then a gunshot fired.

Nightmarish images flashed from her dreams.
Run!

She forced her eyes open. Her gaze darted from corner to corner of the shadowy room. It was darker than before. Was it night?

She fingered the bandage wrapped tight to her head. Tried to read the clock on the wall across from the bed. To remember anything more. But the time, the details around her, wouldn't come into focus. Neither would the past. Nothing remained but the fear.

She felt the pressing certainty that time was running out. She had to get back to... Something... Someone...

Robert kept insisting she was safe. But safe from *what?*

The clock's hands shimmered into clarity—*ten minutes to eleven.* Morning? Evening? What day of the week was it? She didn't have a clue.

The ache behind her left eye throbbed harder, kicking her medication's ass. She closed her eyes, and the nightmare wormed its way back.

Shadows.

Exploding pain.

A gun pressed to her forehead. A child's scream.

Lexi!

"Run!" She startled awake, fighting her unknown attacker.

Fighting nothing but air.

Footsteps rushed into the room. One touch, and she knew it was Robert. She found him leaning over her. Her hand was already in his, and she had no idea who had reached for whom. And she didn't care. It was a fantasy, that he'd always be there for her, but she didn't care.

"There's nowhere to go," he soothed. "No need to run. You're safe."

With his words came more bits of nightmare. Lieutenant Downing's insistence that she remember and let him help. That she was someone named...

Lexi.

She was fighting Robert's hold now, suddenly hating the safety he brought with him. He said something into the intercom above her bed.

"I have to get back...." Time was running out. "If I don't get her out, he'll..."

"Who?" Robert asked—the question making her struggle harder, because she lost the answer before her mind could grab on to it. "If you don't get *who* out? There's no one here but me. The police are staying in the hall where they belong. It's just me, Jane. Try to relax."

"The apartment..." She had to get to... Get to where? A fuzzy image formed in her mind. "Near the mountain...over the bakery...wait for Bambi's call..."

Bambi?

The picture her brain played next was from an ancient black-and-white cartoon about a cat.

Felix?

It was official.

She'd lost her mind.

A nurse bustled in with a syringe, heading for the IV bag.

"No!" She had to stay awake. She had to remember something that made sense.

"It's only a mild sedative to keep you calm." Robert squeezed her hand. He nodded to the nurse, who was dressed from head to toe in cotton candy pink. "Your brain's not ready to handle all of this yet. Slow down until the memories come on their own. Let me help you."

Let me help you.

The lieutenant had said that, too.

Another wave of anger took over.

"Get away from me!" She pulled free of Robert's touch.

Words like *trust* and *safety* were scarier than the nightmare.

"Jane?" Robert took her hand again.

"Leave me alone."

"I'm not going anywhere." The sedative was helping his touch feel right again. "I'll be here when you wake up," he promised.

As the room faded around her and the drugs took over, she realized she believed him. And that was the scariest thing of all.

CHAPTER FIVE

"WHERE'S ALEXA?" Evie's father asked for the hundredth time.

She looked up at him standing in her bedroom's doorway. When he'd unlocked the dead bolt from the outside, she hadn't moved from where she was reading on her bed. When he'd opened the door, she'd clutched Felix closer and pretended to keep reading her latest novel about flying dragons and the magical kids who controlled them when the grownups around them couldn't.

But as soon as she'd heard his voice, she'd lost the ability to pretend he wasn't there. No one ignored her father. It was starting to look like Lexi had been afraid of him, too, and Lexi wasn't afraid of anyone.

"Answer me when I speak to you," he ordered.

He might have been asking her to make up the rumpled bedcovers. Or asking one of his goons to eliminate a threat to one of his schemes. Didn't seem to matter. His demands always sounded the same.

What came next was always the same.

"I don't know where Lexi is," Evie insisted. It had

been two days, and nothing. No rescue. No Lexi. "She's gone. She's not coming back."

Just like her mom.

Always the same.

Lexi wasn't dead, somehow Evie was sure of it. But had her friend forgotten about her promise? Had she left Evie for good?

"You seemed to think she'd come back when you tried to call her."

The night Si and Am had disappeared, too. The night she'd decided to be brave, and her father had banished her to her bedroom and hadn't let her out since. And now he was on the inside of the locked door...

"I was wrong," she whispered.

Of course you were wrong, Felix rasped in her ear.

The stupid stuffed cat had started talking to her again, just like before Lexi had come.

I won't let him touch you again, he mocked in his best "Lexi" impersonation. His happy little cat grin smiled away, while he laughed in her head. *She lied. I'm the only friend you have. Why do you think she was taking you away without me?*

"You were wrong about what?" Her father stepped closer to the bed.

Evie swallowed, clinging tight to Felix.

"I was wrong to trust her." She tried not to believe it, but the numbness was already washing through her. Her fingers tingled when he took Felix and tossed the cat on the table beside the bed. "I was wrong to trust anyone but you."

Her father and Felix.

They were all she had.

"Good girl," he said, not meaning a word of it. He was still pissed. He'd heard no news on Lexi's whereabouts and was convinced Evie knew more than she was telling him.

So tell him! Felix screeched from his perch beside the bed, only it wasn't really a screech because Evie could barely hear him now.

Her father's fingers ran through her hair.

"You're Daddy's good girl, aren't you?" he asked. "You'd tell me if you knew where Alexa was."

"Yes."

Except good girls didn't have conversations with their stuffed animals. And good girls didn't talk their nannies into running away with them. And good girls didn't block the world out with make-believe friends and kiddie movies, while their fathers did things fathers shouldn't do.

But the world was fading faster, along with her father and Felix and the secrets she knew about Lexi. Evie let go, needing the numbness, needing "being good" not to hurt anymore. That's what Lexi had promised. A world that was safe. Real. No more make-believe.

But Lexi had gone away, just like everyone else. And maybe she really wasn't coming back.

"Good girl," her father said as the room misted to white. "Give Daddy what he wants…."

Always the same, Felix crooned, his whiney cat voice the last thing Evie heard…

"FBI?" ROBERT was seething. He was standing just outside Jane's room, and it was entirely possible his blood was boiling. "I walk down the hall for some coffee, and when I come back the FBI has barged into my patient's room!"

"He had an order from a judge," Nurse Beckham explained, not the least bit intimidated by Robert's tantrum.

Nothing intimidated the woman. Her fearlessness made Deirdre one of Robert's favorites…most days.

"A court order to harass a critically injured victim?" So much for Downing feeling protective toward his *witness.* The man had called in the federal authorities. "I don't care if someone has a hall pass from God, I said no one was allowed in there!"

Five minutes. Robert had been gone five lousy minutes.

Through Jane's windows, he could see some guy who wasn't Downing—a hard-around-the-edges character in a conservative suit—leaning over Jane's bed for a nice, friendly chat.

"I didn't *allow* him to do anything." Deirdre crossed her arms over her ample chest. *Jackass,* the frown on her face added. "I told him to get the hell out, then I paged you. Then I paged Dr. Washington.

You're the big dog on this floor. You want him out before your boss gets here, have at him."

She chuckled as Robert marched into the room, as if to say, *this ought to be good.*

"I need you to tell me what you remember," the man was insisting to Jane.

"You need to step away from my patient," Robert challenged.

The agent flipped a badge from his belt without turning around. "FBI business. I'm going to have to ask you to leave until—"

"I don't think so."

Jane was groggy but awake, and she looked terrified without really looking at anything or anyone. She was propped up on pillows, closed in on herself, clutching the blanket to her chest.

"Your patient's in danger," the agent countered.

"Of you slowing her recovery?" Robert crossed his arms over his chest. "I would have to agree."

"Keep interfering the way you have with Lieutenant Downing, and she might not live long enough to recover."

Jane's gaze jerked to the agent's, then to Robert's. Robert stepped closer, reaching for her.

"You're safe here in the hospital," he assured her.

Out in the hallway, an angry Downing was scowling through the windows.

"Is that how you felt living with Dmitriy Andreev?" the agent pressed. "*Safe?* How 'bout when his men caught you running from one of his warehouses and started beating on you? Any of that sounding safe to you?"

Jane's breath rushed in and didn't release. Her chest rose and fell in jerking motions while she fought to breathe. Her pulse raced beneath the fingers Robert curled around her wrist. She shook her head from side to side, her pupils dilated.

"Take it easy." He rehooked the oxygen feed beneath her nose—the oxygen she hadn't needed since yesterday. "Breathe for me."

Nothing.

Her heart rate stumbled into a too-fast, uneven rhythm. Alarms sounded. Deirdre and another nurse hustled in, followed by Seth.

"Midazolam," Robert ordered.

"No medication," the agent insisted, "until I've finished my interview."

"Unless you're an expert in postoperative brain swelling," Seth warned, "or you're *trying* to induce enough anxiety to cause a seizure, this is Dr. Livingston's call. I don't care who signed that piece of paper you waved under my staff's nose."

"Midazolam," Robert barked without looking up from the woman shaking in his grasp. "Stat!"

Jane wasn't just shocked at whatever the FBI agent had said. Her terror was jagged-edged. Raw panic. Robert was shaking, too, while he waited for the sedative to do its job.

Jane Doe was just another victim of random street crime, his ass.

Who was Dmitriy Andreev, and what the hell had happened to this woman?

Dmitriy!

The name ricocheted inside Alexa's head like a kaleidoscope of razor-sharp glass, spinning in all directions. Consuming everything. Unbearable. Impossible to stop.

Dmitriy...

Evie...

Oh, my God, Evie!

"Let me go!" Alexa fought the hands holding her. Robert's hands.

A doctor who had no idea that she wasn't a vulnerable victim he could save.

Dizziness rolled through her. She braced herself against the weakness. The need to trust someone, anyone, so she wasn't alone. She pushed back against the pain and the memories. The truth her mind had hidden until she'd heard Dmitriy's name.

Now it was all back—every speck of it.

Robert reached to cup her cheek. She flinched away, hating how much she craved his gentleness. Hating the dream she'd let too close when she hadn't known better. Hating him, because now he was part of her nightmare.

The IV line feeding whatever they were giving her pulled tight, pinching the vein in her hand. She started to yank the thing free.

Robert wasn't having it. "Don't. Calm down. Let me help you."

"Get your hands off me." Tears were spilling free, clouding her vision.

Tears? Letting more emotion in wasn't going to fix this, or save a little girl who'd become Alexa's biggest mistake.

Sometimes you have to let yourself be weak, in order to find your true strength, her mother's voice reasoned.

Alexa ignored it as she reined herself in, focusing on carving out an escape plan instead. Cool, calm logic was what she needed, not motherly advice about the finer points of letting herself be vulnerable.

Then she realized she was clinging to Robert's hand. That she couldn't let it go, or see his face clearly anymore.

"What... What did you give me?" She covered her mouth against the shock of how defenseless she still was. "Oh, no..."

A small plastic basin appeared beneath her chin.

"Try and breathe, Jane," he said. "That's all that's important right now."

Jane?

Breathe?

On a choked laugh, she lost the last of her dignity and whatever was in her stomach. Robert cradled her head, and she let him—mostly because she lacked the strength to do anything else.

Mostly.

Meanwhile, the still functioning part of her brain

used the diversion to peek at the suit still standing where he'd been when she'd woken up.

Agent Crimmons.

"I can't be here." She slumped back to the pillows, flinching. She hadn't meant to say anything out loud.

"You can't be anywhere else," Robert countered. He raised a cup to her lips. Water—paradise—trickled over her tongue. "And no one's getting back in here tonight, so calm down."

"I still need to talk with her," Crimmons insisted.

Alexa couldn't get her eyes to open again. She couldn't remember how many people were in the room. How far it was to the hallway. How many windows. How many doors. Useless details she'd been trained to track. Information she'd need to get out of the hospital and back to Evie.

She had to make enough sense of things to figure out what to do next, and that meant everyone had to believe she still couldn't remember.

Even the doctor who, in her dreams, had been her angel.

"You need to step back out into the hall," Robert instructed Crimmons.

"I don't think…" she whimpered. She made a weak attempt to pull away from his touch. When he wouldn't let go, squeezing her fingers instead, her next whimper bubbled up from her soul. "I can't…"

You can't lose it like this, Alexa!

But the weakness, the darkness, was winning again.

"...my boss has already..." Crimmons was saying. "...federal government's policy..."

"...don't really give a damn..." Robert replied.

"...key witnesses...top secret investigation..."

The men kept talking, but the words stopped making sense.

The mind-numbing pain was gone at last. Along with it, her revulsion for the world she'd tried to flee. Memories of the brutal bastard who was still out there, hurting people. Thanks to Robert's drugs, all of that could wait.

But the drugs weren't all that was numbing her mind so completely, so fast. Robert hadn't let go. His voice, challenging Crimmons, was close. Warm. Understanding. Having him near took away the impulse to run, and that scared her more than anything.

She should be fighting to get out of there. Instead, she clung to Robert's hand.

He was her surgeon, nothing more. Useful, as long as he protected her from Crimmons's questions. But as the room and his touch faded, she held on tighter.

His voice rose above the white noise filling her head.

"I'm not going anywhere," he insisted. "You're okay here. I promise."

And she let herself believe him, even though she knew being okay couldn't be real for her. Not yet. Her head fell to the side. A familiar face looked back from the other side of the window.

Rick.

No, "okay" wasn't even close to what would be waiting for her in her nightmares.

CHAPTER SIX

SETH FOUND HIMSELF in his office, in the unenviable position of standing between his chief of neurosurgery, and the FBI operative Robert looked ready to tear limb from limb.

"The federal government!" Robert paced a few feet away, then back. "Why does the federal government care about a mugging victim?"

"Not your problem." Terrance Crimmons matched Robert glare for glare, then turned his stare on Seth. "I need unrestricted access to the patient, and I expect your assurances that she won't be medicated again until I have her statement."

"What you need isn't this hospital's concern," Robert insisted.

Crimmons regarded Seth in silence, waiting.

"According to the FBI assistant director I just spoke with—" Seth headed behind his desk "—a federal judge has made it our concern. That court order is legit, Robert."

And Seth would follow it to the letter, no matter how much he'd like to help his friend pound some sense into Crimmons.

"A court order saying what?" Robert sounded less like a doctor by the second.

Seth had seen neurotic family members behave less territorial.

"Unless the patient's health is in immediate danger," Crimmons explained, "I am to have your staff's full cooperation for however long I deem it necessary to my investigation."

"Investigation into what, exactly?" Seth asked before his friend could. "Judge or no judge, this is still my hospital. I have a right to know if treating a patient is exposing my staff to undue danger."

"We have no reason to believe there's any threat to either the patient or Atlanta Memorial staff, but—"

"Is that why you've had police camped out in ICU for two days?" Robert demanded.

Seth waited for Crimmons's answer.

"You just said she wasn't in danger," Robert pressed.

"It's a possibility," Crimmons allowed. "That's why we're monitoring her room, but—"

"But what you're really concerned about is the information Lieutenant Downing failed to get," Robert challenged.

"The patient's safety is our top priority," Crimmons insisted.

"Naturally," Seth said. "Safety from what?"

The agent's response was another protracted stare, colder than the last one. "The information we're seeking is critical to—"

"The patient doesn't even know her own name."

Robert planted his hands on his hips. "Amnesia is usually temporary, but if you keep pushing—"

"Are you certain?" Crimmons couldn't have sounded less convinced.

"Am I certain of what?"

"That she can't remember?"

It was Robert's turn to stare, the question Seth had been asking himself for the last half hour clearly just sinking in.

"You're saying," Robert sputtered at Crimmons, "that she's faking the dangerously high heart rate and cognitive disorientation that resulted from you shoving your way into her room?"

"I'm saying, why should she be scared to talk with me, if she has absolutely no memory of why I might be here?"

"He has a point." Seth winced at his friend's *eat-shit* glare.

"I need to know if she said anything to you just now, before you put her under," Agent Crimmons demanded. "Whatever she said, no matter how unimportant it might seem to you."

Robert inhaled, then let his breath out slowly. "Who is Dmitriy Andreev?"

Crimmons slowly shook his head.

Robert scowled at Seth's nod to answer the agent's question.

"She said *I can't be here,*" he answered. "Now tell me who this Andreev character is you wanted to ask her about."

Crimmons dismissed him.

"What's your best estimate on when she'll be awake next?" he asked Seth.

"Each patient's reaction to medication is different," Seth hedged. "I can't give you a definite time, but I'll instruct the staff to alert you the moment she comes around. You can question her, as long as her condition remains stable. But if you put her health at risk again—"

"I assure you," Crimmons said, "your patient's welfare is as important to us as it is to you."

"Whatever you want from her is all that's important to you." Robert ripped the office door open and stalked out.

Seth's go-to surgeon, calm and in control in every crisis.

"If he's going to interfere with my investigation," Crimmons said, raising an eyebrow, "perhaps he should be replaced by another doctor."

Seth smiled for the first time since reading the agent's court order.

"Robert Livingston is the only reason your *witness* has recovered so quickly. Two days post-op from a surgery this extensive, the average patient would still be in a pharmaceutically induced coma. Jane Doe has not only repeatedly regained consciousness, but her responses to the brief neurological exam Robert was able to give her were remarkable."

"All the more reason to let me push for the information we need, so I can leave her to recover in peace."

"Except pushing too hard could reverse her condition dramatically."

"Meaning what?" Crimmons looked genuinely nervous for the first time.

"That Robert's the best man I have—the best on the East Coast—at finessing the art that neurosurgery becomes, once science has done all it can. There's still serious risk of brain swelling, blood clots, stroke. We're talking about a severely traumatized patient. Back off for another twenty-four hours and let my man do his job. Certainly, that little amount of time couldn't be a problem."

"And after twenty-four hours…"

"I'll assess the situation, and if need be personally make sure your piece of paper from that judge is followed to the letter." If Robert didn't manage to get his act together by then. "For now, be grateful that Dr. Livingston's following his instincts and doing what's best for his patient. He's a professional, just like you. Let the man do his job."

WHEN ROBERT marched past Downing on his way to Jane's room the lieutenant looked ready to explode himself. A part of Robert didn't give a good damn. The part that needed to check on Jane and ignore her ever-present bodyguard. But what he needed wasn't the point. He stopped and returned to the man's side.

Both Kate and Seth had accused him of being too emotionally involved with this patient. One glance at Downing's expression convinced Robert that he wasn't the only one. Mindful of all the reasons this was a bad idea, he made sure they were far enough from the other officers not to be overheard. Then he inched closer, invading the personal space of a man who seemed to be contemplating the best place to pound his rather intimidating fists.

"I'm starting to think," Robert said, keeping his voice low and trusting the instincts that had never let him down, "that we're the only ones around here putting Jane's well-being before anything else."

Downing scanned the hallway himself. He nodded.

"Maybe it would be more productive to work together," Robert reasoned, not even sure what he was suggesting.

But an ally in this craziness was an ally. Too bad his *ally* had, to date, been as cooperative as a pit bull after a week-long fast.

"I'm listening," Downing said, though Robert could have sworn the man's mouth didn't move.

"I get that I can't know the details, or Agent Crimmons would have the reason he wants to throw my ass in jail." Robert was reassured when Downing smirked, then subtly relaxed. "But I think you know why whatever Crimmons said in there scared Jane. I believe you know her somehow, beyond being the one who found her at the scene."

Seconds passed. The lieutenant seemed to be running a list of pros and cons in his head.

"I'm listening," he said again.

Fed up with the cloak-and-dagger shit, Robert pivoted toward Jane's room.

"Wait," Downing said behind him.

Robert stopped. He sighed, wondering if he really had lost his mind. But he waited, for Jane's sake.

"You're right," the lieutenant said just above a whisper. "There's a lot going on here that you can't know about. But if I could just talk with her, maybe..."

"Maybe what?" Robert turned back. "Maybe you can push her and get whatever information Crimmons couldn't? Become the hero of this little farce?"

"No." There was no anger in the word. No pit-bull snarling this time. Downing sounded desperate, not spoiling for a fight. "Maybe I can find a way to reach her without hurting her even more. Maybe I can help you protect her, before Crimmons gets another crack at her."

"And she'll listen to you, because..." Robert wasn't angry anymore, either.

Or skeptical.

He believed every word coming out of the other man's mouth. But he was still totally in the dark, and that wasn't a place he'd hung out in for a long, long time.

"Because if she would just remember me," Downing explained, "she'll know that she can trust me, the same way she trusts you for some reason."

A backward dynamic Downing couldn't hide his distaste for.

So they were both floundering in the dark while they stood between her and whatever Crimmons wanted.

Robert felt himself nodding. Accepting what had to be done. There was something stirring around a defenseless woman they both cared about. And they were equally determined to do whatever they could to help her.

"I intend to make sure her blinds stay closed from now on," Robert announced. "I don't want the slightest thing to disturb Jane while she rests, or to startle her when she wakes up in—" He checked his watch, gauged the strength of the dosage he'd given her. Then for good measure, he added an hour to his estimate. "In about six hours."

Downing glanced at his own watch.

"You've been here going on three days without sleep by my count," the lieutenant observed. "Your boss is dealing with Crimmons. There's no reason for you to lurk by your patient's bedside for the next six hours. Unless—" the bull dog scowl returned "—you still don't trust me."

"If I didn't trust you," Robert snarled back, loud enough to be heard at the nurse's station, "I'd have *your* ass, and your men, thrown off this floor. You people are the ones who aren't listening. Whether she's in danger or not, I'm that woman's doctor, and I'm the one responsible for her well-being while she's in my care. *You* need to start trusting that."

"Oh, she's in danger." Downing's lips flattened. "Removing my men would be the biggest mistake you could make."

"Then I suppose you'd better stay," Robert conceded. "I'll be back in six hours, at which time I expect my patient to be resting comfortably. Do whatever you have to do. Sit inside with her to make sure no one else gets in, if that's what it takes. If Crimmons or anyone upsets Jane, I'll be notified. And I'll be more than happy to clear this floor of everyone but medical personnel."

"Well, we wouldn't want you to be happy, now would we, Doctor?" Downing glanced over Robert's shoulder, nodding at one of his men's chuckles.

Robert left without a backward glance, trying to believe he was leaving Jane in good hands.

Ally or not, good idea or not, giving Downing access was the only card Robert had to play at the moment. That and figuring out everything he could about Dmitriy Andreev, before he faced Crimmons again.

CHAPTER SEVEN

"THE RACKETEERING indictment against Dmitriy Andreev, the suspected head of an Internet organized crime ring responsible for embezzling funds from several international banks from Moscow to...was dropped today after the judge ruled there was insufficient evidence to continue the trial...."

Robert clicked his computer's mouse, pausing the video clip of a two-year-old news broadcast his search engine had dug up. FBI agents... Round-the-clock APD watchdogs... A form of organized crime he'd never heard of... And all of it centered around his patient...

Patient?

She's in danger, Dr. Livingston....

Robert gave up. Gave in to the unprofessional feelings he shouldn't still be having for Jane, and the fear that came with knowing that she was mixed up with a dangerous man like Andreev.

He'd lied to Crimmons. Despite Jane's panic and the damage any stress could do to her recovery, there were sedatives that would allow her to regain consciousness but not be overwhelmed by her situation. He could have Jane awake and ready to talk with the authorities by later that afternoon, but—

I can't be here....

She'd remembered something. Enough at least to recognize on some level that she really was in danger, long before Crimmons and Downing had confirmed it. Would remembering more put her in more danger from the mob? From the FBI?

"Isn't that the same dress shirt you wore yesterday?" Kate asked from Robert's office doorway.

"No." He clicked the Internet connection closed and rolled down his cuffs, then pivoted his chair to face the music. "I have several in the same color in my desk. I've been showering and shaving here the last couple of days. Sleeping on the couch."

"Days?" His ex sat in a chair across from his desk. "You haven't been home since she got here, have you?"

"Nope."

Nothing unusual about that. He slept at the hospital from time-to-time, when his surgery schedule got out of control.

Except Kate would know Robert's schedule had been cleared indefinitely. Something he'd never have allowed before.

Before Jane.

"And now you and Seth are trying to snow the cops about your mystery patient's condition." She shrugged when he didn't respond. "Seth had me paged, filled me in enough to ask me if I knew anything about your attachment to your Jane Doe. Of course I told him we hadn't spoken in weeks. Then I popped into her room to check her chart. I found an APD officer hovering at her bedside just now, waiting for her to wake up."

"Yeah." Robert leaned back in his chair instead of elaborating. "So, you're thinking the midazolam was overkill?"

"Not if you're worried about protecting the woman from questioning, more than you want her brain active so the nurses can monitor her recovery."

Silence filled the distance between them while he weighed the help he needed against the instinct not to trickle more of the situation's insanity into the lives of people he cared about.

"Is there any way Stephen or Martin could quietly dig up some information?" he finally asked. "Say, hypothetically, on a defendant in a federal case that was dropped a couple of years ago?"

Kate was newly married to one of the top lawyers in town. And her brother, Martin, a former sheriff's deputy, taught at the police academy.

"Jane Doe?" Kate asked.

Robert shook his head. "Some guy the feds want to question her about."

"Feds?"

"APD is just window treatment. There's an FBI agent running the show, and he's not telling Seth any more than he has to. All I have is a name, someone Jane's supposedly associated with, and what little I can find out about the guy isn't reassuring."

Kate started to speak, stopped, then sighed.

"What's going on, Robert?"

"I need to know more about Dmitriy Andreev."

"The man the FBI wants to question your patient about?"

"I'm not sure *question* is the right word."

"Neither is *patient*, evidently."

"Nope." Robert didn't have the energy to argue. "She isn't."

He'd been up for days. He'd made an embarrassing display of himself in Seth's office. And when he'd left Downing the opening to talk with Jane, he'd trusted someone he'd been ready to challenge to a fistfight just a few hours ago. At the moment, Kate chewing him out for losing his cool over a patient ranked dead last on Robert's list of worries.

"So, what exactly is she?" Kate asked.

Robert's mind hadn't stopped circling that question since he'd last seen Jane. Touched her. He kept returning over and over to the same inconvenient, impossible truth.

"She's someone I need to help." He shook his head at the inadequate description.

"More than you need to help the rest of your patients?" His ex's voice held that hard edge she rarely indulged in. Her gaze sharpened. "Because lying to the cops and dragging Seth into this... Once the jig is up, you'll be fighting to save both your careers."

"If that's what it takes, it's worth it! As long as Jane is safe."

And in that instant, just how much Robert was willing to risk for the woman became crystal clear.

"She's completely vulnerable," he explained. "Someone has to care enough about her, to put caring for her first—no matter what she's gotten herself into with this mob character."

Kate nodded, a bemused flicker of approval softening her *you're nuts* frown.

"Well then." She smiled. "I guess it's lucky for Jane Doe that *care* is a word that doesn't scare the pants off her neurosurgeon anymore."

ALEXA KNEW she wasn't alone the moment she woke. The same way she finally knew she was *Alexa*. Both realizations were so startling, she didn't have to fake being still. For several seconds she couldn't breathe.

"Lexi?" asked the person she'd sensed sitting beside her.

She'd never before experienced disappointment and relief in the same flash of an instant. It wasn't Robert—the angel from her dreams she'd wanted to be there. But the man beside her *was* the person she needed to talk with, if she was going to get herself out of the latest mess she'd made.

"Lexi?" Rick took her hand. Held on tighter when

she flinched. "You're awake. I can tell. I've always been able to tell. Open your eyes."

I've always been able to tell...

Classic Rick. His familiar, smart-ass bossiness washed over her. He was the bratty, almost–big brother she'd never been able to shake. And she'd never really wanted to.

She blinked her eyes open. Blinked harder when she saw his smile just inches away. The comfort of it, the memories, swamped her. Feelings that wouldn't have gotten to her before Evie.

Before Robert.

Rick thumbed a lone tear from the corner of her eye.

"Do you remember me?" he asked.

The fact that he had to ask was a testament to whatever control Alexa still maintained over her faculties. Either that, or she'd lost it so completely that she'd thrown him.

She inhaled.

To stall, yes, but also to clear her head. Rick had already put his career on the line once, when he tried to extract her and Evie from the warehouse without authority. Did she dare drag him into her mess even further?

"I'm sorry if I'm frightening you." He tentatively squeezed her fingers.

Too tentatively for a man who could move like lightning and intimidate with a mere glance. When she didn't shy away from his touch, the tension along his jaw eased a bit.

"When the other man was in here earlier, questioning you, I was watching from the window. You reacted so violently to what he said. Almost like you…" He stopped. So careful. So worried. "And then you seemed to recognize me when you saw me through the window…."

She couldn't look at him anymore.

She couldn't lie to him.

Not to Rick.

"You do remember." His finger under her chin turned her head back toward him. His expression hardened with even more worry. "What are you playing at, Lexi?"

He'd asked her that when she'd sent him the emergency extraction code over her secure cell line. Him—not Crimmons. She hadn't been playing then, either.

"Maybe I'm trying to keep your well-developed posterior out of what I'm doing, for your own good." She tried a smile and felt it wobble. "The single ladies of Atlanta would never forgive me if I didn't."

He smiled, too, his chuckle full of relief and affection.

"Damn, you scared me." He brought both the chuckle and the smile under control. "You're still scaring me. Why the hell won't you talk to Crimmons? Or your doctor? Livingston's putting his job on the line protecting you, and he doesn't have the first clue what's going on. Why all the cloak-and-dagger now? It's over."

She eased her chin away from his touch.

"Lexi," he cautioned. "It's over."

"Good." If she'd had the strength, she'd have punched him in the arm, like when they were younger. "Glad we've got that cleared up."

"Oh, my God." Rick pushed from the chair, stomped several feet away and turned back. He looked just like his dad always had, when one of them screwed up big-time. "You think you're going back? Your head was bashed in, Lexi. Andreev's men would have shot you dead if I hadn't shown up when I did. You…"

His voice caught. His eyes grew mysteriously moist.

"Rick, don't." She'd never seen him lose it like this. Never even thought it was possible. "This is my problem. You don't have to—"

"Stop it, Lexi!" He scraped the heel of one palm across the corner of his eye, concern giving way to fury. He stepped back to the bed. "You called me to pull you out. Then you didn't even wait for me to get there. What where you thinking! You were a bloody mess by the time I made it to you. The element of surprise and those goons having to deal with that screaming kid are the only reasons they didn't finish you off. But now that you're awake and have a decent chance of surviving this with your gray matter intact, you want back in?"

"I don't have a choice."

"Whatever evidence you've collected isn't worth it," he protested, being her friend instead of the hard-nosed cop she needed to help her through this.

"It's not just about the evidence." Though Dmitriy had to be stopped. "I—"

"You still have one foot in the grave." Rick planted his palms on either side of her shoulders, trapping her. "Tell Crimmons where you stashed whatever you collected and—"

"No. I'm going to be out of here long before Crimmons realizes I've remembered anything."

"What?"

She pushed against Rick's chest and tried to wiggle free. Finally she made it an inch or two higher on her pillows. But she felt her own useless tears building again. Streaks of pain and nausea throbbed outward from the battered side of her head.

She fought not to react to any of it. Not to feel anything.

"I'm getting better by the second," she challenged. "And—"

"And you didn't even know your own name this morning! You're not going anywhere. All I have to do is talk to Crimmons, and—"

"And I'll never speak to you again."

Rick.

The closest thing to family she still had.

Could she really walk away from him for good? Did she really have a choice? Her determination must have registered, through the shock of her threat. Rick sat. Braced his forearms on his thighs, his head hanging.

"It's the girl," he said to his feet. "You're not going to stop until you get the girl out."

Evie.

"I can't leave her there, Rick." For Evie's sake, Alexa had to make him understand. "I need to figure out what to do next. How to get back to her. And I can't do that here. Not now that I'm awake. Crimmons will keep pushing to interview me. He'll realize I have my memory back, and then I'll have lost my chance."

"Chance to do what?"

"Finish this disaster the way I should have in the first place. Help me, Rick. I'm going to get back to Evie. Maybe not today, but I'm going to get stronger, and then I'm going back in."

She held her breath and prayed for just a speck of the luck her mother had promised she could make when she needed it most. Alexa had never needed a second chance more, not even when she'd been fighting her way out of that alley.

Rick shook his head as he stared at the floor, refusing to look at her. Still, she knew what his answer would be before he spoke. Just like she'd known she could trust Robert Livingston with her life, with her dreams, long before she'd remembered who she was.

Rick was where her secrets had always been safe as a child. Robert was evidently where her messed-up mind thought they could hide now. And she had no choice but to leave them both behind.

Knock it off! Get away from the doctor, before you lose the ability to get away at all.

"I know you risked your job to help me before," she admitted. "I'm sorry for asking you to do it again."

"Did you think I wouldn't!" Rick looked up then, pissed and scared. "Do you really think protecting my badge is what's stopping me now?"

"I won't ever ask you for another thing," she pleaded. "Just help me get out of here. I have somewhere to go. All I need is a little time to clear my head."

"Then I'll take you there. And when you're ready, I'll bring you back in to see Crimmons."

"No. You've put enough on the line for me."

"Lexi—"

"I'll be fine on my own, believe me. And you can believe I'll find a way out of here whether you help me or not. You know I will."

"I know I'm going to regret this," he said to the floor, then he sighed

But he was nodding again.

Thank God.

"Tomorrow," she said through the light-headed relief that screamed how weak she still was. "I should be ready to go tomorrow...."

EVIE GRIPPED her can of soda tighter. Told herself not to cringe when her father stepped behind her kitchen chair and smoothed a hand down her hair.

"I told you," she insisted. "I don't even know if Lexi is alive. One of your guys hurt her—" A hiccuping sob made her drop her head.

Her father's fingers snagged in her hair. "I don't

believe you, my darling. I need Lexi back, and so do you. Why won't you tell me the truth?"

"I…" She'd never seen him so worked up for so long. "I told you, I heard a gunshot before they dragged me into the car and brought me back here. Lexi was already hurt. That's the last time I saw her. There were police everywhere. I don't know anything else."

"But you know how to reach her," he answered smoothly. "Don't you?"

Evie shook her head and sipped her root beer. She squealed when he yanked her head back by her hair.

"Your nanny gave you a number to call if she had to leave. Now why would she think you needed something like that? And why would my people not be able to trace the call you made?"

"I…" Fizzy soda fired its way down Evie's throat. The burning spread through her chest. She swallowed it, but not the nervous cough that came next. "I don't know."

He braced his hands on the table, on either side of her, leaning forward and trapping her beneath heat and muscle. She should have known this was coming when he let her out of her room. She shouldn't have trusted him to forgive her. She never should have trusted Lexi, either.

"How long has she known?" her father cooed in her ear, as goose bumps rippled like terrified little bubbles, racing down her arms and away from his calm voice. "How long did it take for you to betray me?"

Betray *him?*

Evie stiffened, her head making contact with his chin. He hissed, but for once she didn't care what he did next.

"You mean how long did it take your *lover* to figure out that I was the reason you couldn't get it up with her?"

Evie was whirled around so fast, the kitchen kept spinning long after her father pinned her to the table.

"What did you tell her!"

"I didn't have to tell her anything. Everyone knows." But Lexi had been the first person in the mighty Andreev organization to care. To tell Evie that she had a choice. That there was a way out of the numbness and the make-believe. "You're the only one around here oblivious to the fact that you're a freak."

"Where was she taking you!" His eyes were wild, his accent heavier. "She was paid to work for me and to keep you entertained, not steal you away from me. What did she tell you!"

"She said I don't belong to you!" Lexi had been crying. She'd found out the secret that everyone eventually learned, and it was like everything had changed overnight. "She promised you'd never touch me again!"

Lexi had promised hope. *Bambi,* safe to run free and not be afraid of the hunter ever again.

"Alexa promised?" Shock rumbled through the chest that was too close. "Alexa's a computer hacker. I'm your father. *My* promises are the only ones that matter."

He rounded the table, his anger melting into parental concern.

"How could you have believed her, Evie? She's a worthless little whor—"

"She was your girlfriend!"

"Because she was smart and creative with my money, and more than willing to cover for me being a... What did you call me? A freak?" The fabric of his silk shirt expanded and shrunk with each breath. "She's a nobody. I knew you were too attached to her. That's why I was taking you back with me to Europe this time."

"Taking me with you?" Evie grabbed Felix and stumbled out of her chair, toppling it as she backed away.

Her father's widening smile stopped her before she ran. She wouldn't get far, and he'd enjoy making her pay for trying.

"Alexa was starting to know too much. I couldn't have that, especially how she was keeping you away from me. Once she finished her last project, I was going to cut her loose."

Cut her loose?

"Lexi wasn't—"

"She was stealing you away from me!" Her father's shouts, his hatred, always brought the numbness back.

Tell him, Felix hissed. *Forget covering for the stupid nanny.*

"It was my idea," Evie lied, the same as she had before, when they'd been in her bedroom…on her bed…. Any second, she was going to throw up. "I begged Lexi to take me with her. She didn't want to."

Her father's head tilted to the side. The tiniest motion. His eyes narrowed.

"Take you with her where, Evie?" He was closer, when Evie could have sworn he hadn't moved.

He looked evil now, just like every villain in her cartoons.

"I—I…" She swallowed her stutter. Tried to believe Lexi was coming back for her. *Bambi… When you call, say that you're Bambi and leave a message for Thumper….* "I don't know."

Liar! Felix screeched.

"Just like you don't know what happened in that alley?" The hunter ran his fingers through Evie's bangs, then a blur of motion was her only warning before he backhanded her to the floor. He smiled down as she cradled the side of her face. "If Alexa's still alive, I'll find her, my darling. Lying to me's not going to change that. I need her to finish her work, and you're going to help me make sure she does. Then I'll find wherever she was planning to take you, and wipe it and her from the face of the earth."

"I'm not ly—"

"You're mine, you ungrateful bitch! No one takes away what's mine. Alexa's coming back for you, and then she's mine, too. Maybe I'll let you watch while I explain a few realities to her. Would you like that?"

Evie shook her head, crying. Hoping. Believing in Lexi still, while Felix screamed that there was no chance anyone could stop the hunter.

"It'll be for the best." Her father knelt and shoved Felix away. The room started to fade around them. "I tried to protect you," he said sadly, "but you have to see. You have to see what happens to people who take what's mine, my darling. You'll see, when Alexa comes back. Then you'll understand why you can never leave me. It'll be for the best...."

CHAPTER EIGHT

ALEXA FIRST became aware of the smell of food, then the fact that she couldn't remember when she'd fallen asleep the night before. The aroma of bacon and eggs infiltrated her confusion, piercing the vagueness. Then a wave of hunger hit from out of nowhere. The kind of hunger she suspected had tempted trapped animals to gnaw off a limb, to get to whatever tempting morsel had lured them in the first place.

"You're licking your lips." A warm chuckle made each word sound like a smile. "Open your eyes, and we'll see how you do with solid food."

Floating in the moment, Alexa felt herself smile back. Her lips were stiff. Her eyes were too gritty to open, and the overhead lights were blistering her corneas through her eyelids. But how often did a woman get breakfast in bed from an angel…?

Breakfast in bed?

Angel?

The lingering wisps of drug-induced nothingness evaporated. She opened her eyes to find herself still in ICU, with Robert Livingston sitting beside her bed. He'd been there every time she'd woken, ever since Rick had left.

She checked the wall clock.

"Don't you have a job to do?" The croak in her voice ruined the put-down she needed her words to be. She had to get away from the pain meds. Her mind had to stop hoping Rick would be there every time she drifted back from a drug-induced stupor.

"Until further notice, *you're* my job." He pushed the awesome-smelling tray of food closer. "The nurses tell me you nixed Atlanta Memorial's five-star Jell-O and mashed potatoes yesterday. How about a few bites of something more substantial?"

Did the man have to look so adorable, sitting there smirking and competing with the food for which could make her drool the most? But she'd need her strength, today of all days, so eating it was. She pushed farther up on the pillows. Her head didn't appreciate the maneuver. When she would have sunk back to the bed, Robert's hand supported her shoulder.

"Take it slow," he cautioned. "We'll get you a bit more mobile today, but let's take it slow."

"Mobile sounds good." *Slow,* not so much.

He spared the doorway a wary glance. He'd brought her meal tray in himself. He'd kept the windows covered to shield her from the view of anyone walking down the hallways outside her corner room. There wasn't a nurse in sight.

He was protecting her. Like the angel from her dreams.

Ditch him! Him and your fantasies.

Eat, if it makes him leave faster, then get out of here!

She reached for the lid covering the food, but her arm gave up halfway to the tray. She sighed while Robert finished the job and scooped up a small bite. He held it up for her to sample. She willed her hand to take the fork and feed herself the eggs—at least, the half of them that didn't dribble onto her hospital gown.

He started to brush the mess away, smiling, while the barely there feel of his touch feathered across her collarbone. Her breath stalled. The room shrunk around them. He slowly withdrew his hand, his gaze sharpening, heating, while he shook his head in disbelief.

Energy arced between them. He was suddenly no longer a doctor acting more attentive than she had any right to expect. And she was no longer a patient needing his medical help. She needed him.

"I…" she muttered. "I'm sorry, I…"

"No need to apologize," he said gruffly. "I…"

But he didn't seem to know what to say, either.

What's wrong with you!

Somehow between the dreams and the nightmares, the voices in her head and the confusion, Robert had become something her mind had let itself need. Every touch had been telling her exactly that. Every time she'd woken and been relieved to find him beside her. Now, with her amnesia no longer protecting her and him still sitting so close, her addled brain was determined to hang on to the dream.

Her fingers reached to trace the stubble sprinkled along his jaw. Her body clenched and melted when that jaw tightened. When his eyelids lowered at her touch.

It was the drugs. It had to be the drugs. She didn't fantasize or lose herself in ridiculous moments of insanity.

Keep your focus on your goals, her mother's voice whispered from the past. The same voice that had been chanting for days about waiting for the moment to be right. *Figure out what you really want, then go for it. Then nothing can stop you.*

And what Alexa wanted was away from this man and his hospital. Only her head was lifting, her lips hovering just below Robert's. She had to know. She had to have just one memory with him that wasn't a dream, before her disintegrating life took over completely and she never saw him again.

Robert gripped her shoulders. His gaze trailed a scorching path to her mouth.

"Jane." A guttural groan followed. "I'm your doctor. I can't—"

"My name's not Jane." Her lips trembled against his. She felt his body shudder. "And I want a new doctor."

"Damn."

Robert's mouth took hers.

His hands slid in a too-gentle path down her

shoulders. He pulled her closer. One touch of his tongue, one shared breath, and she was shaking. Then he was inching away, cursing again.

"We can't," he whispered. "You don't need more confusion on top of everything else. You can't even remember who you are...."

He cut another glance toward the closed doors, analyzed the readings on her monitors—all in the amount of time it took her brain to convince her hand to smooth up his chest, so she could cling to his lab coat to keep him close.

Her. Clinging!

It had to be the meds. The stupid dreams.

But it had been so long since she'd let herself need anything beyond working her way out of Dmitriy Andreev's insane world. Saving Evie. Maybe somehow saving herself. But in Robert's arms, the rest faded. She could lie to him, lie to herself, about everything else—but not how he made her feel.

"Please." She shivered at the roughness of his hands covering hers. "I don't understand it, but your eyes... Your touch. They feel better than anything I could possibly remember. You make me feel free of all of this. Please... Please don't stop."

Knowing she shouldn't, knowing she had commitments to keep—promises she'd made to her mother, herself, Evie—she kissed him and let herself forget one more time.

He was there. He'd been there through every

minute of the fear and the pain and darkness. And he was still standing between her and danger, even if he had no idea how much trouble she was leaving him to deal with.

His kiss filled her with the sweet need for more. So she clung to his shoulders. Shuddered at his taste, and the simple goodness of a good man needing her back. She'd lost so much of herself, long before the amnesia. But Robert drawing her into his arms was a glimpse of what life could be like without the darkness. Something clean and simple and honest she wouldn't have to run from to keep herself and everyone else safe.

"Jane," he whispered in her ear, his lips trailing across her jaw.

Alexa.

She wanted to hear Robert call her Alexa. She wanted...

She had no business wanting any of it!

She couldn't be there a second longer....

Call me...

Alexa broke free and tried to move away. He pulled back, still holding her shoulders. His gaze was troubled, and for the first time wary.

"We need to talk," he announced in his doctor's voice.

Still breathing hard, he released her and stood. His hand brushed at the wavy, dark hair she'd run her fingers through. Then he cleared his throat, all business again.

"There's no chance I'm going to be able to keep them out of here today," he said.

He didn't bother to explain who *they* were. Or that he'd exhausted the tests he'd been running to keep Crimmons at bay.

"How much do you actually remember?" he asked.

She rubbed a finger over her bottom lip instead of answering, wiping at the tingling his kisses had left behind.

"APD? FBI? Organized crime?" he asked. "Any of it starting to ring a bell? Dmitriy Andreev's name certainly made an impact the other day."

She stared up at him.

Her doctor. Her protector. Of course he'd sensed the truth.

He watched the heart monitor blip out the anxiety she'd normally have kept under control. Then he removed the leads from her chest, the blood pressure monitor from her arm and every other wire hooking her to the array of space-age monitors charting stuff she wondered if anyone really knew how to read.

"I can't help you," he said. "Not if you won't level with me. That kiss… The way you've been acting since the FBI got here… You're upset about something, but you're afraid to tell anyone what it is."

He'd insisted she could trust him from the very first day. And she obviously did somewhere deep inside. The same way she trusted Rick—only differently. Robert was kind and concerned and loyal, just like Rick Downing. But the connection she felt to him went far deeper.

All the more reason she had to leave.

"You can't do anything but get yourself hurt." She dropped the weak-patient act. "Thank you for your help, and I...I'm sorry about the rest.... But I don't want you to put yourself at risk."

She'd practiced getting in and out of bed with Rick. Walking several steps. She'd been shaky. Nauseous. Weak. But it had been enough to convince her she could do this on her own.

She had to do this on her own.

"Why would being your doctor put me at risk?" Robert asked.

"You can't tell me it's good for your job, hanging around here babysitting me." She looked away from those knowing eyes.

"Why don't I believe that my job is what you're most worried about?" He studied her from the foot of the bed. "Who's Lexi?"

She sat taller and jerked her breakfast tray closer, angry at herself. Angry at him.

Why did he have to be there this morning? Why—why!—had she let herself reach for him, when too much was riding on her being able to walk away free and clear?

"Tell the FBI they can come in," she said. "But first, I'd like to choke down some of my breakfast."

Robert's hand stalled hers in the process of lifting another bite. He'd slipped back to her side, just as deftly as he'd slipped beneath the barriers that normally kept her safe from wanting and needing anyone.

"What kind of trouble are you in?" He looked so solid. So ready to understand and help her.

"Trouble you don't want any part of." She made a fist beneath his touch, around her fork, and waited for him to back off.

"So, you *do* remember." He sounded dug in, despite her warnings.

Another damn thing to admire.

"Yes." She laid the fork down and swiveled away from him, her legs dangling off the edge of the bed. Did the floor *have* to keep looking a mile away from her feet? "I remember all I need to about trouble."

"And when was the last time you remember letting someone help you?"

She slid to the floor, waited three beats to make sure the ground didn't yank itself from beneath her, then she set out, leaning on the IV stand while she shuffled.

"I do what I have to do," she answered. "Now, if you don't mind, I need to use the restroom."

Of course he was by her side in an instant.

Of course it felt like he'd been there forever.

"I'm—" he began.

"My doctor."

Her *doctor* caught her the second her knees buckled.

"You wanted a new doctor, remember?" His smile was a dangerous thing.

More dangerous than falling into Dmitriy's world. More dangerous than letting a damaged fourteen-year-old so close to her heart, Alexa had started feeling again. The kind of feeling that nearly got both Evie and her killed.

And if Robert didn't listen to reason, things weren't going to end much better for him.

"I want you to let go of me." She kept shuffling.

She had to remember what was important. Bambi and Thumper. And, of course, Felix.

No more distractions.

No one else being hurt because of her.

She put one foot in front of the other. Robert stayed with her until they reached the bathroom door. Stayed close as she grabbed the support bar installed in the wall.

"Can you buy me some time to pull myself together, before I have to face the federal music waiting outside?" she finally said, asking for his help yet again.

Needing someone is a hard thing, honey, the long-ago voice admonished.

Thanks for that, Mom!

"Sure, no problem." Robert stood just outside the bathroom door, giving her space that should have felt good. "I can let go of helping you, too, if me being involved is making this harder."

It was exactly what she'd needed him to say. More than she deserved, when she'd been the one who'd reached for him. So why was she grappling for a firmer stranglehold on the steel beneath her fingers, to keep herself from reaching for him again?

"It sounds like steering clear of being involved is something you know a little about." Her voice was shaking.

"I'm familiar enough with it to know when someone I care about is freezing *me* out."

"You..."

It was either sit or fall at Robert's feet. She made her way to the closed toilet seat.

"You care?" she sputtered, once the stars stopped circling her vision like they did in the cartoons Evie watched too often. "You don't know the first thing about me."

Robert knelt in front of her, like the prince in the fairy tales that fueled little girls' dreams.

"I know enough. Andreev's a dangerous character. However you're mixed up with him, I'm betting the cops are more concerned with nailing a mobster than they are protecting you. It sounds to me like you need—"

"Some privacy." Distance. A spine. *Get away from this guy.*

Robert nodded, calm as ever and so damn tempting.

"I can probably buy you an hour." He edged away. "I'll send in a nurse to help you back to bed."

"No, I'll be fine."

More than fine.

"I'll believe you're *fine,* once you're back in bed." He leaned against the doorjamb. "So, it's either going to be me or a nurse helping. Do you need to use the bathroom or not?"

Alexa stood up instead of answering, wary of the rising anger beneath her angel's level tone. Making a scene would only attract the attention of everyone in the hallway. He helped her back to bed as efficiently and with as little personal contact as possible—the same as he would any other patient. Then he headed for the door, looking back one last time.

"Goodbye, Jane," he said before letting the thing swing shut behind him.

Needing someone is a hard thing, honey....

Exactly why Alexa didn't let herself need anything. Why it was time to shake off the meds and the stupid kiss and the stupid dreams and start eating the breakfast that was suddenly turning her stomach.

She ripped the IV from her arm, wincing at the sting, and pressed the washcloth she'd smuggled from the bathroom to the dribble of blood seeping from the wound. Bypassing the eggs and bacon, she fingered the dish of buttered toast. Then she shoved that plate aside, too, jostling a plastic cup of juice and dousing a piece of paper folded beneath that she hadn't seen.

She reached for it, instincts screaming not to. It was a drawing. She could see the bleed-through from the Magic Marker on the inside. Evie's love for bright colors blinded Alexa as she opened the rumpled paper.

It was a picture of Bambi and Thumper playing in a clearing near the base of a mountain.

Free.

Safe.

Remember me, Lexi was scribbled in red marker at the bottom of the page, in fourteen-year-old Evie's too-childlike handwriting.

You're mine, Alexa had been written over it in black pen. Dmitriy's block script. *Come back to me. Don't make me come for you. Don't do that to Evie.*

"BREAKFAST!" Crimmons demanded half an hour after Robert left his patient.

The patient who'd kissed Robert senseless, then written him out of her life.

"Managing solid food is an important step to your witness being medically cleared," he insisted.

And Robert wasn't moving away from the door a second before the hour he'd promised Jane was up.

Crimmons's stare strayed to the APD bodyguards around them. "Do you honestly think solid food is what's important right now?"

"That," Robert responded, "and the fact that short of bodily removing me, you're not going to win this round, yes."

Meanwhile he was losing Jane, or whatever her name really was.

Like you ever had her in the first place.

"The patient can't regain her strength without proper nutrition," he lectured. "This is the first interest she's shown in food since waking. I fail to see how waiting another half hour will impact whatever investigation you need her help with."

Lieutenant Downing had revealed nothing after

spending several hours with Jane yesterday. His impassive stare from over Crimmons's shoulder revealed nothing now. But if Robert's instincts were right, Jane had her memory back. Which probably made this Robert's last chance to help her.

Crimmons's thin smile guaranteed it.

"Stalling my work is only going to cause more trouble for your patient, Dr. Livingston." The agent followed Robert's eye-line, sent Downing a silent snarl, then swung back to Robert. "She can take another half hour for breakfast. Fifteen minutes for a nurse to extract more blood or fluff her pillows. Maybe a few more for someone to give her a bubble bath. But today's the day. My speaking with her could be—"

"A matter of life or death?" Robert finished for him.

Instead of responding, Crimmons turned to Seth, who'd just joined them. "How long will the patient be dining?" he asked

Seth plucked Jane's chart from the plastic holder beside the door and kept walking. "If I could have a word with you, Doctor."

He stopped several feet away, flipping through the records and waiting for Robert to join him.

"I know what you're going to say." Robert took the chart and closed it. "But she—"

"She's no longer in medical danger. It was a good ploy, and it bought her another day. But I just received a personal call from Crimmons's judge—who's going to have both our butts in jail for contempt if I let you interfere with whatever's going on a minute longer. You can observe, but Agent Crimmons is in. There's nothing more I can do about it."

Which meant there was nothing more Robert could do, either. Crimmons's grin was the genuine article this time. The man opened Jane's door and walked inside. Robert tensed to follow, but Seth's palm cuffed his shoulder first.

"What!" Robert rounded on him.

"Back off. This is a crappy situation," Seth sympathized. "But maybe it's for the best."

"You didn't see her earlier, when she begged me for time to—"

"What the hell is going on!" Crimmons bellowed from inside.

Robert rushed into the ICU suite, Seth on his heels.

CHAPTER NINE

ESCAPING DOWN the back hallway, through the door Rick had made sure was unlocked and unmanned, had been almost too easy for Alexa. Finding the stairs he'd said would be close by, working her way down to the fourth floor and finding the janitor's closet he'd left clothes in—along with keys to an unmarked car—had been a bit tougher.

But leaving Robert, after she'd run him off and used his unwitting help to distract Crimmons, had turned out to be the hardest thing of all.

Sitting on a cracked plastic chair, a haze of narcotics and relentless pain sapping at the strength she'd been so sure would hold up, she forced one leg then the other into mint-green scrubs and pulled the voluminous pants over her hips. She stripped off the backless hospital gown with arms that felt like overcooked pasta and dragged the boxy top over her head. Then she forced the image of Robert's final concerned expression out of her mind.

She had to forget the feel of his strength drawing her in. The compulsion to pull him closer. The lure of his voice, coaxing her awake, reassuring her that she wouldn't be alone.

Focus on Evie's drawing.

Focus, period!

She struggled into the ratty pair of one-size-too-small sneakers that had come with the clothes. Breathing deeply in and out, she forced herself to her feet. A check of the hallway through the smallest opening she could make with the door, and then she was heading toward the stairwell, expecting to feel one of Crimmons's men at her back with every shuffling, excruciating step.

But, so far so good.

She stuck close to the wall on her way down, using the railing to keep her on her feet. Maybe no one would think a patient recovering from brain surgery would be stupid enough to tackle stairs. That had been Rick's response, when she'd asked him to scope out their location.

Whoever decided ICU should be on the tenth floor deserved a special place in hell, besides the other people who'd made her life a slice of heaven on earth.

Just a little farther.

She'd be safe once she was outside.

Yeah, right.

Like she'd kept Evie safe?

The car keys Rick had left were digging into her hand. She loosened her grip and grabbed for the keyless remote, looking down to find the right button.

Please, God, let the car not be too far away from the stairwell.

Have to keep moving.

Ignore the pain.

Do the job.

Focus on Evie.

But it was Robert's face she saw again, as the stairwell door slammed shut behind her. And, she suspected, it was the fact that she was leaving him farther behind with each step that had her heart racing faster— not worrying whether she'd find the car as she pressed the key fob. The headlights of a Camry parked only a hundred feet away flashed in silent welcome.

Thank you, Rick.

Robert's smile, not Rick's, answered in her mind while she slid into the leather interior, his concerned eyes tilting at the corners with a hint of a smile.

Knock it off, Alexa!

She had to make it out of the parking deck before she passed out. She should already be gone. There was no time. Crimmons would have a team scouring the place for her.

So, take the car out of Park.

And she did, even though she was leaving an avalanche of federal trouble at Robert's feet, no matter how good a surgeon he was or how much weight he pulled at Atlanta Memorial.

SETH TENSED beside Jane Doe's empty hospital bed while Robert and Agent Crimmons squared off, Lieutenant Downing joining in for extra punch.

"It's not my fault APD decided not to watch both doors to her room," Robert said.

Crimmons scratched the twitching muscle in his jaw. "But it *was* your decision to stall my interview, so your patient could escape—from a room where you've insisted the blinds be drawn for the last eighteen hours. Have I mentioned yet that interfering with a federal investigation is a felony?"

"Once or twice." Robert had never sounded more cool. Cold, actually. Furious. "Do you really think I give a damn about your investigation, when a patient recovering from a life-threatening injury just ditched her round-the-clock medical care to get away from you!"

"What I *think* is that you're personally involved with your patient, Doctor. A patient that's been a wild card the Bureau hasn't been able to trust for over a year. And now a scum like Andreev might just walk, when he should be going to prison."

Over a year?

"You son of a bitch!" Robert wedged his forearm into the agent's throat and shoved him against the nearest wall. "You've known who she is all along."

"Shit!" Downing got to the pair before Seth.

"Back off!" Crimmons growled. Robert's hold only allowed him a whisper, but the agent made it count.

Seth and Downing stalled.

Crimmons's smile should have been a warning, but Robert was clearly only seeing red.

The agent's knee came up first, striking pay dirt. Then a quick tap of the flat side of his hand to a pressure point on Robert's neck and some kind of Hollywood-worthy twist to Robert's wrist, and Robert was on his knees, his arm bent behind his back, head down while his breath wheezed in and out.

"Do you have any idea what you've done, Doctor!" Crimmons growled into Robert's ear. "You and your *patient* are in more trouble than your fancy title and medical degree will get you out of. I strongly suggest you find yourself a lawyer."

ROBERT HAD NEVER seen Atlanta Memorial's executive conference room packed with so few medical staff. Him, Seth and Kate, and that was it. And Kate had had to fight her way in to sit beside her lawyer husband.

Stephen Creighton had agreed to protect Robert's rights the best he could, even though the man's skills as a legal-aid advocate seldom veered into finessing felony charges. But Robert had seen him in action. Stephen was who he wanted by his side. And Robert wanted his ex-wife there, too. Even Seth, though his chief of staff looked angry enough at the moment to help Crimmons string Robert up.

These people were his family—that had never been more clear. A support network that had closed ranks around him, whether he'd asked for it or not.

And now, if he was going to keep helping Jane, he'd need every last scrap of their support.

Lieutenant Downing stood to the right of the door, revealing nothing each time Robert caught his attention. Two of his officers were flanking the entrance from the outside. Crimmons and a man who'd been introduced as a federal prosecutor sat across the table from Robert's group. Several other suits accompanied the pair. None of them had offered an introduction.

As if Robert cared if he was on a first-name basis with his lynch mob.

"If your client is prepared to cooperate and tell us exactly what he knows," the federal attorney said to Creighton, "the government might rethink indicting both him and this hospital with conspiracy charges."

"Conspiracy to do what, exactly?" Stephen asked. "Dr. Livingston is responsible for your witness still being alive. Local authorities and federal operatives not being able to keep up with her whereabouts has nothing to do with him."

"The doctor and his chief of staff obstructed federal and local law enforcement from accessing an asset to an ongoing investigation. They've tied up the operations of a joint task force it's taken years to assemble, just when it's in a position to achieve its objectives. Their actions might have negated the team's last chance of bringing down its target."

"Asset?" Robert's mind flashed to an image of the

flesh-and-blood woman the attorney was objectifying. "Bringing down a target?"

"Robert—" Seth and Kate cautioned at the same time.

"No!" He shook off the hand Kate laid on his forearm. "Let me make one thing perfectly clear. I had nothing to do with my patient leaving my care. And I'll bet a year's salary I want her back here just as badly as Agent Crimmons does—even if it means delivering her into your clutches."

"We're trying to protect her, *Doctor.*" Crimmons said Robert's title as if he was trying to get rid of a foul taste in his mouth.

"By pumping an innocent woman for information, when your *team* screwed up protecting her?" Seth asked, speaking for the first time.

"What makes you think we screwed up?" Crimmons polished off the comeback with a deadpan stare. "Or that she was an innocent bystander in the incident? The woman you've been treating is Alexa Vega, and she's been cooperating with the Bureau for years."

Robert caught Downing shifting his feet by the door. Something feral flickered in the glare the man shot toward Crimmons.

Alexa.

Robert pushed to his feet, his fists pressed, knuckles down, onto the table. "You were hounding her long before she got here. Your *operation's* the reason someone hurt her. And you're still dogging

her, because whatever she has on this Andreev char-
acter is more important to you than her safety. My
God. No wonder she kept screaming in her sleep.
What's wrong with you people!"

"Sit down, Dr. Livingston," the gray-haired agent
to Crimmons's left said. He folded his hands and
waited. Crimmons and the federal attorney waited
with him. "I'm the special agent in charge of a joint
strike team investigating a cyber-organized crime
syndicate that operates out of Russia. Our investigation has led us to criminal activities we hope to link
to targets living in the Atlanta area. With your
attorney's permission, I've been authorized to share
what few specifics I can, in exchange for your cooperation while we find the patient you've known as
Jane Doe, before she injures herself further."

"So you can get the information you need from
her," Robert spat back.

"Sit down, Robert," Stephen insisted. The
lawyer's leather chair creaked. He studied both
Crimmons and the man who clearly held his professional leash.

"Mr…?" Stephen waited.

"Special Agent In Charge Donovan."

"SAC Donovan," Stephen continued while Robert
sat and ran a hand through his hair. "What specific assurances are you offering my client and this hospital
in return for Dr. Livingston's cooperation?"

Robert looked down at his hands.

They were shaking. His hands never shook. Not

during the most challenging surgeries. He closed his eyes. The memory of *Alexa's* pale, determined features came into focus. He clenched his fists against the thought of never seeing her again. Of being too late to keep her from hurting herself beyond the point where even his skills could repair the damage.

"I'll cooperate," Robert said before Donovan worked up the interest to speak.

"Robert—" Stephen cautioned.

"Absolve the hospital of all responsibility for whatever you think I've done to your precious investigation, guarantee me that returning my patient to this hospital is your top priority and I'll tell you whatever I can."

Silence claimed the room. Each side of the table seemed to be trying to read how much it could trust the other. Crimmons looked like a man hunting something to shoot with the gun holstered beneath his suit coat.

Donovan was the first to blink.

"Done." A good-ol'-boy half-smile replaced his glacial negotiating stare. "We realize that it's not your fault you didn't know what you were dealing with, Doctor."

"Exactly what was he dealing with, then?" Stephen asked. At Donovan's hitched eyebrow, he shrugged. "How's the good doctor to know what you need, without a frame of reference to go by? My sources tell me Dmitriy Andreev is connected to

Russian mafia. So he's *made*. That doesn't make him stupid. His interests are mostly intellectual property—extortion, fraudulent gambling sites, identity theft. Most of his operations are handled in international jurisdictions U.S. authorities can't touch. Why does an Internet banking hacker rate a joint APD and Department of Justice task force? And what's so important about a battered woman who can't remember her own name?"

Robert and Kate shared nearly invisible smiles at her husband's cool rendering of the details. As *families* went, Robert's was kicking butt—even if Seth's normally calm expression tipped toward a snarl every time he looked Robert's way.

"If her memory's still compromised," Crimmons challenged, "why was Dr. Livingston working so hard to keep us out of her room? Did Alexa remember something you don't want us to know, Doctor?"

"Would she have been safer not remembering?" Robert made himself not glance toward Downing.

He still couldn't be sure what the other man's involvement was, or if he'd really been on Alexa's side at all. Robert did, however, suspect that Downing was a large part of the reason she'd disappeared under everyone's noses. And he wasn't about to give the man up. Not yet, at least.

"Let's start with this," Robert said. "What makes you so sure she remembers important information about Andreev?"

"You mean besides the panic attack she had when I mentioned his name?" Crimmons's narrowed gaze sliced through the bull. "What did she say to you!"

Donovan held up his hand for quiet. Robert smiled as Crimmons gritted his teeth.

"If Dr. Livingston's patient would be at risk if she talked with you—" Stephen cleared his throat "—then any concern he may have over revealing something she may or may not have said would be understandable."

"Listen." Crimmons pointed his trigger finger at Robert. "You self-righteous—"

"Your patient nannied for Dmitriy Andreev's daughter." Donovan's hand returned the other agent's to the table. "Through intelligence we've collected monitoring the household, we have reason to believe she tried to run with the child on the afternoon she was injured."

"Injured?" Seth challenged.

"The woman came close to having her brains bashed in." Robert shuddered at the memory. Then what hadn't been said registered. "She wasn't just running with the kid, was she? She was running toward something. Your protection, by any chance? What happened? Your men showed up too late, and she was left to fend for herself?"

Help me…. You have to help me get out of here. We need to go….

Bambi… Have to go back…

"Why was she running with the child?" he demanded.

"Our intelligence suggests that Evie Andreev might have been in some form of danger from the father."

Robert blinked at Donovan's emotionless delivery.

"In danger, as in abuse? Physical? Sexual?" When there was still no response, he pressed on. "Let me guess. That detail's not within the parameters of your operation's focus. You only agreed to help the nanny kidnap the child, because of whatever information she had on the father?"

"I assure you, the child was a complete surprise to us."

"You expect me to believe you weren't in contact with Jane—Alexa—before she ran? That a nanny got it into her head to run with the daughter of an international mobster on her own? What, and the APD just happened to be there to stop the guy's goons from finishing her off!"

Donovan was already shaking his head. "I'm not at liberty to discuss the situation any further."

"That's what you used to trap Alexa into spying on her boss, wasn't it? Your promise to help with the child."

Donovan's stare chilled, becoming as blandly hateful as Crimmons's.

"I can assure you there was no coercion. Ms. Vega was a willing participant, and our intention was never to put either her or the child's well-being in jeopardy."

"If Andreev's so dangerous, what made his nanny

think she could get away with spying for the federal government?"

"Who said anything about spying?" Donovan's good-ol'-boy demeanor was back in spades.

Just the inspiration Robert needed.

"Don't 'aw shucks' me." He shrugged off Kate's hand again. The hell with staying calm! "You're a *special agent in charge—*"

"Robert—" Creighton grasped Robert's forearm when Robert rose to his feet.

"You want something from this woman," Robert continued. "Badly. Atlanta Memorial has been swarming with police and probably your operatives since she hit the E.R. with injuries you didn't protect her from. Now she's my patient. Her recovery is *my* responsibility, you son of a bi—"

"Robert!" Seth was on his feet, too. "Sit down and give your attorney a chance to help you, before you make even more trouble than you already have."

Robert stayed standing. He stared down first his best friend, then the men seething across the table from them. He shoved his hands into the pockets of his lab coat, the fingers of his right hand closing around the child's drawing he'd found beside Alexa's bed after the agents rushed out to look for her.

Remember me, Lexi.

You're mine, Alexa. Come back to me. Don't make me come for you. Don't do that to Evie.

"Explain to me why I should trust you with anything

Alexa might have said to me, when she couldn't even trust you to help her protect an abused child?"

"Allegedly abused," Donovan corrected.

"Explain it."

"The maximum time you could spend in jail for obstructing a federal investigation? My pleasure."

"That won't be necessary." Creighton pulled on Robert's arm until Robert was once more sitting beside the lawyer. "What information, exactly, do you need from my client?"

"Whatever he knows that could help us pinpoint his patient's whereabouts, so we can return her for treatment. That shouldn't be too difficult, should it?"

"Her recovery has been the least of your concerns up 'til now." Seth glowered a warning to *shut up!* Robert's way. "My staff has an obligation to ensure the best treatment possible for our patients. That's what Dr. Livingston has been doing."

"Whatever information she escaped with is no good to us, Dr. Washington, if she's medically in no shape to turn it over. We both want the same thing— Alexa Vega's satisfactory recovery."

"Heartwarming." Robert felt cold everywhere at once. "Explain your connection with my patient, and I'll tell you whatever I can."

Donovan sighed, then nodded once…toward Rick Downing.

The lieutenant took a step closer. The scowl he shot Donovan barely achieved respect. For Robert, he managed resigned apology.

"Alexa Vega has contacts within the Atlanta Police Department," he said. "And—"

"She's a cop?" Robert asked.

"No. But when we discovered her access to Andreev, our joint initiative with the APD was helpful in identifying—" Downing sent another pointed look Donovan's way "—key people from her past. An officer who could reach out to her."

"We offered her our help getting out of a dangerous situation," Donovan continued. "In return for whatever details on Andreev's Internet operations she could bring us. Only she ran with the child before the appointed extraction time, and we have no idea what happened before the officers arrived at the scene."

"Or what information she managed to grab," Robert added.

"She's a lucky woman that she got out at all. And since then, we've done everything we can to conceal the fact that she's alive. Now, it's only a matter of time before a very angry, very well-connected mobster catches up to her. Help us help her, Doctor. Help us bring her back here where she's safe."

Back to the hospital where she'd been so certain she couldn't trust anyone, she'd run? Not just from the agents and Downing, but from Robert, too.

The apartment, get to the apartment.... Near the mountain...over the bakery...

Wait for Bambi's call...

Robert had no idea what most of what she'd

said meant, but he'd bet money that he knew someone who did.

Every eye in the conference room was focused on him, while he absorbed who Bambi and Thumper most likely were and how much trouble Alexa Vega was in. He glanced briefly at Downing, caught his almost imperceptible nod, then focused on Special Agent in Charge Donovan.

"Of course," he agreed. "I'll tell you everything I know, though I'm afraid it's not much. Ms. Vega was sedated the majority of the time she was in my care."

CHAPTER TEN

ALEXA GLANCED at herself in the Camry's rearview mirror and shrieked in her mind. Letting the scream out would have finished melting what was left of her brain.

Okay, a scary-eyed, bride-of-Frankenstein-haired woman with a head swaddled in cotton gauze might attract a bit of undue attention in a quaint, conservative mountain village. She closed her eyes and rested her forehead against the steering wheel. The twenty-minute drive from downtown Atlanta to historic Stone Mountain felt as if it had taken hours.

You can't sleep in the car....

You can't sleep in the car....

Open your eyes!

She did, slowly, wincing at the blast of winter sunlight awaiting her. She carefully slipped the *Dynasty*-esque sunglasses she'd found in the console between the front seats back on, then gingerly donned the *Bahamas Baby* straw hat that had been sitting in the passenger seat—probably souvenirs abandoned by one of Rick's girlfriends after a weekend quickie to Paradise Island.

Cadaver eyes and post-coma coif neutralized, the next trick was ditching the car where it wouldn't draw attention, then somehow making it up the stairs that led to the apartment even Rick didn't know about.

Fifteen minutes, tops.

You can do this.

You can do anything.

Those had been her mother's last words to her, as she'd assured Alexa she could move on from losing her. The last words of a brave woman, who had been so certain her daughter would follow in her footsteps.

Instead, Alexa was weak and sick and needing to be back at the hospital with Robert holding her hand and standing between her and what she had to do next. She'd never felt less like the hero her mother had thought she could be.

"WHERE IS SHE?" Robert demanded the second he was free of the FBI's questions and managed to corner Lieutenant Downing privately.

Downing walked farther into the break room near Seth's office, away from the hallway door.

"What's your interest in the matter," the lieutenant asked, "now that she's no longer your headache?"

"What's my interest…?" Robert drew a blank. He'd been half expecting the same runaround he'd gotten from the feds. "I'm genuinely concerned about her."

"Concerned?"

"Alexa's well-being is important to me."

"Important?" Downing nodded. "So Crimmons wasn't so far off base, when he suggested that you have more than a professional attachment to your patient's case."

"Why do you need to know?" Robert took his turn asking.

"Because before I even consider answering a question I'm not supposed to know the answer to—"

"You weren't supposed to help your witness run from this hospital, either," Robert reminded him. "But my money's on you getting Alexa what she needed to make a break for it. Not to mention brainstorming it all with her while I made sure you two had alone time in her room."

Downing inclined his head in agreement. "If you're sure that I know more than I'm saying, why not confront me in the conference room? Crimmons would have been all over me."

"Because..." Robert had to see her again, away from this place. Away from everything and everyone that was terrifying her. He had to reach her, somehow... "Because I truly want to help her."

"And Donovan and Crimmons and I don't?" the lieutenant asked.

"You know, you say that...." *Careful,* Robert reminded himself. *You need this man's help.* "You say that almost like you've done more with those agents than deliver Alexa when they needed a contact in Andreev's household."

The lieutenant didn't jump to defend himself, or get angry, or any of the other things Robert might have expected. Instead, he walked to the counter cluttered with coffee cups and other flotsam found in every break room Robert had ever been in.

"Alexa kept rambling about cartoon characters," Robert said. "Bambi and Thumper and Felix the cat. All of them meeting near a mountain…"

In response, Downing riffled through several drawers, before he pulled a creased take-out menu free and grabbed the pen from his uniform shirt pocket. He scribbled something at the bottom of the page, then turned back.

His closed expression gave nothing away. He handed the menu to Robert on his way out of the room.

"I've known Alexa Vega most of my life," he said just inside the closed door. "Anyone who does anything to hurt her is going to answer to me, I don't care what the FBI thinks they're in charge of."

Warning shot delivered, Downing left Robert to study the menu in silence. Robert ran his thumb over the address jotted in the bottom corner of the page.

Now all he needed was a legitimate excuse to cover his absence from the hospital. Because no matter how skillfully he'd BSed his way out of that boardroom, he didn't believe for a second that he was off the FBI's radar.

ALEXA ABSORBED the absolute quiet of the apartment and gave herself a moment to feel safe. A crash outside sent her crouching near the one window that fronted the parking lot, until she realized the sound was from a garbage truck emptying a nearby Dumpster.

Okay.

Moment over.

She pushed to her feet and started making plans that she couldn't while Crimmons had been breathing down her neck. She didn't have long. Didn't dare stay past the morning.

She'd sleep. Pass out was more like it. Then she'd find something to eat. Whatever it took to get her ready to move on—once she'd decided where *on* would be—and before Andreev or the FBI caught up with her.

But first things first.

She stumbled to the answering machine. Collapsed into the chair beside it. Pulled off the ridiculous hat and glasses and pressed Play.

"Um… This is…Bambi. I…I'm looking for Thumper. I need…I need to talk to her. I need…Felix and I need to—"

A gasp followed.

Rustling and a squeal.

The line went dead.

The recording stopped.

So did Alexa's heart.

Evie.

She'd called, three days ago according to the digital display on the machine. Alexa buried her head in her hands.

She was too exhausted. The pain was getting too bad to ignore. She couldn't move another inch, but she had to get back to Evie.

The girl's drawing materialized behind her eyes. Her message. Dmitriy's demand. His threat. It all jumbled together in Alexa's mind. She had dropped the note in her rush to get out of ICU—leaving behind more than enough evidence to tell Crimmons or Donovan, whichever man found it, too much.

Idiot!

You'll figure it out, her mother's voice countered. *Give yourself time to get it right.*

Alexa had been eleven and working on her algebra homework, and she'd been frustrated by something she hadn't understood in class. Her mother had, of course, been telling her not to be so hard on herself. That they could figure it out together.

She fought the memory, but unconsciousness was coming whether she wanted it or not, sucking reality away. The nightmare would be waiting when she closed her eyes, except this time she'd know for sure it was real. Every bit of it. Her botched escape, because Dmitriy had flown back into the country early. He'd told Alexa to pack Evie's things, because the child was to leave with him that evening—without her. *Daddy* had been anxious to keep his baby with him and away from Alexa.

So she hadn't waited. She'd called Rick in a panic, certain she could get Evie and the evidence away before it was too late.

Her head spinning, she pushed herself to her feet and made it to the bed. Lying down on top of the covers, she fingered the blanket almost beyond her reach until she could pull it over her and let herself fall.

Sleep.

She had to get some sleep.

You're safe... a gentle voice whispered as the world slipped away. *You're not alone. I'll be here when you wake up.*

Robert's voice.

His face, his gentle eyes and the passion of his kisses were the dream waiting for her this time, not the face of a monster and the screams of a terrified little girl. Everything was going to be okay. Somehow.

In her dreams, they'd figure it out together. Robert would be there when she woke up.

CHAPTER ELEVEN

SETH LOOKED UP from the mound of paperwork he'd yet to touch that day and groaned at the pissed-off expression on his visitor's face.

He almost regretted paging her.

Almost.

"You suspended Robert!" Kate demanded.

"He didn't give me a choice." Seth dove into his administrative nightmare, signing his name furiously to one form, then the next.

"You need choices?" Kate stomped into the room, all long legs and blond determination, clothed in pediatric scrubs. Yellow bunnies hopping all over her. "Well, let me see…backing up your best friend and not suspending him would have been another way to go."

"The man is self-destructing. He thinks he can control everyone and everything around him like he does his O.R."

"He's falling for a woman he knows nothing about, and he's spinning."

"Yes. You know that. I know it. Everybody in the hospital knows it by now. I don't care how cooperative he was in that boardroom, he gave the FBI nothing to go on. If he stayed on site, they'd keep hounding him for more. He'd have gotten an up-close-and-personal look at the inside of a jail cell by the end of the day. Refusing to cooperate with a federal investigation is playing hardball without a bat."

"He says he doesn't know anything more."

"And I'm not buying it." Seth tossed his pen down and watched it skid to a stop near the fishbowl filled with cheddar crackers. "I'm an administrator of this hospital. If I condone his behavior, the board of directors will get sucked into the legal mess Robert's creating. Doesn't matter how much I want to help him, or how pissed off the entire situation makes me. My only official course of action is to require hospital staff to cooperate fully with the authorities and their court order."

Kate's eyes narrowed. Her frown eased into a hint of a smile. She took a handful of crackers, then settled into one of his guest chairs, curling one bunny-covered leg beneath her.

"So tell me about the *unofficial* courses of action you're considering." She always looked so pleased with herself when she read through other people's bull.

On someone else, it would have come across as smug. But Kate was simply Kate. And when it came to people, she was almost never wrong.

"I was thinking it was damn gentlemanly of your husband to offer to represent Robert on such short notice. I'd take it as a personal favor if Stephen would continue to keep an eye on things. See what he might do to help, if and when things get sticky again."

Kate's smile could light up the room when she put the slightest bit of effort behind it. At the moment, it was like watching a sunrise bloom.

"Stephen's in court the rest of the day," she reasoned casually. "How do you propose he keep an eye on things?"

"You were married to Robert for five years. I don't suppose you could keep track of things for your husband for a while?"

Kate sat forward. "Robert knows where she's gone, doesn't he? He told you to suspend him, to get you off the hook for whatever he's really up to. And to give him a chance to go after her, without being conspicuously missing from this place."

"My agreeing to something like that would have been a conflict of interest for this hospital."

"Of course."

"Robert's going to do what's best for his patient, damn the consequences," Seth added. "But if he's not careful, Donovan and Crimmons are going to know the second he makes a move to try and find their witness."

"Which means…"

"What's the pediatric staff schedule looking like this week?"

Kate studied her folded hands. When she looked up, her nod was so small, he wouldn't have noticed it if he hadn't been totally focused on her reaction.

"You know, Seth." She stood, headed for the door and opened it, so that whomever might be listening in the hallway could catch every word. "I'm not feeling well, and I think we have enough on-call nurses to cover my shift. Maybe tomorrow's, too."

"You should probably head home and take care of yourself, then." He stood, while she managed the weakest cough he'd ever heard. "We go back a long way, Kate. You and Robert are like family to me. Take whatever time off you need to—" she added a sneeze that actually got a chuckle out of him "—take care of things. Let Robert work out his own problems."

"Thanks, I think I will." She winked.

His people never ceased to amaze him. Robert putting his career and maybe even his life on the line for a patient. Kate dropping everything to go after Robert when he needed her help, whether the man wanted help or not.

The two of them had always had Seth's back, while he juggled the insane conflicts that came with his job—giving due consideration to the money and the staffing and the interests of the board and the bank and everyone else standing in line to make a profit off the hospital. All while he stayed dedicated to the quality of patient care. This place was more of a home than Seth had ever known, the same way it had once been for Kate, before she'd met Stephen Creighton.

The hospital had been Robert's top priority, too, before Alexa Vega found a way under the surgeon's defenses.

"Call me if you need anything," Seth said.

Kate gave him one last smile and headed out.

AS USUAL, Robert had gotten exactly what he wanted.

He was suspended from the hospital. Seth and Atlanta Memorial were in the clear, and he was free to focus on Alexa without being under the federal gun.

Well, as free as a man could be, when he was being tailed by the APD or the FBI. Or quite possibly both. Which actually left Robert nowhere, until he figured out what to do next.

Alexa needed pain medication. Aggressive antibiotics. Careful observation for at least another forty-eight hours. New internal swelling at the injury site was always a risk. She shouldn't be moving much at all. A moot point, considering that the address Lieutenant Downing had given him was twenty miles away from the hospital, in a picturesque village where no one would go looking for a runaway nanny.

She needed rest and complete relaxation so her body—and her brain—could heal. But healing was clearly the last thing she planned to do.

He picked up the crumpled child's drawing from his coffee table. Rick Downing hadn't said how much Alexa had remembered. But the child's note scribbled at the bottom of the colorful page, the threat blocked out beneath it, had sent the woman running. She was going back to Andreev's. Robert was certain of it. She'd been fighting to get back to Evie—Bambi—since before she could remember why.

Robert rubbed at the tiny hairs tickling the back of his neck. He'd never been more in awe of another human being in his life. Or more frightened for one. He had to find a way to get to Alexa undetected. He had to talk her out of whatever desperate plan she'd concocted to handle the situation on her own.

His house phone rang. He snatched it from a nearby table and punched the line open.

"Livingston here," he said without checking the display, expecting it to be the hospital calling about one of the cases he'd asked be kept in the loop on.

"How the hell do you expect to help her, hanging out there all day?" a familiar voice taunted.

"What choice do I have?" he spat at his ex-wife, grateful to hear her voice. "I think I was tailed all the way home."

"Too bad we aren't married still," Kate quipped, and she never quipped. Not about their failed relationship. "Hide-and-seek was a whole lot more fun when we were together. Remember how much fun we had that one night?" Kate's laugh wasn't the light, carefree thing it had become since marrying Stephen. But it was convincing enough to play for whomever might be listening in on his calls. "Remember that night? You're a long way from fun and games now, buddy. Seth Washington wants your ass in a sling."

"The feeling's mutual," Robert groused on cue.

"The last thing he told me before I headed home

sick was to let you work through your mess on your own. You must be in deep, Robert, if even Seth won't help you dig your way out."

"You're sick?"

"It's been coming on for days." She coughed like she meant it.

"Then get the hell off the phone and take care of yourself." He made sure he sounded like he meant it, too.

"I just wanted to tell you you're not alone. I wish there was more the rest of us could do, but you've still got people on your side."

Robert checked his watch. He headed down the front hallway and pulled back the sheers shading the front door's glass insets. The cop car was still there. Parked several houses down, but still there.

And somehow Kate had known. She'd told him that morning she was working a double shift today, and she hadn't been sick.

Seth.

He'd have realized Robert needed supplies for Alexa, and a way to get to her without being followed.

You've still got people on your side....

"Hide out for a few days until you feel better." He kept his voice casual.

"You take care of yourself, too, Robert. This will all work out. Everyone's waiting for you to come back once it does, even Martin."

Everyone. Even Kate's brother, whom Robert hadn't seen in nearly a year.

"Yeah. I'm looking forward to it."

After she hung up, he pressed Off.

Everyone, even Martin, who worked half an hour away from the hospital at the Police Training Academy, would be waiting for him to come back....

He peered around the sheers once more. His curbside neighbors weren't going anywhere. So, neither was he, at least not through the front of the house. But there was the kitchen door. His tiny backyard led to the next street over, and a city bus that drove through his exclusive Buckhead neighborhood like clockwork every half hour. Robert could make it to the central APD Training Academy where Martin taught in under half an hour.

Kate. Happily married to another man—the right man for her, this time—and she was still surprising Robert.

Hide-and-seek...

The first year of their marriage, they'd stopped on the way to the hospital to pick up a cake for a staff baby shower. Robert had thought he'd locked his keys in the car when they came back out of the store. In the pouring rain, they'd peered through the windows to no avail, then Kate had begun searching through his pockets. His jacket. His pants. A game that had evolved into their own private party, when they'd taken the bus back home for a spare set of keys, only to stay up all night eating cake and making love and never getting near the baby shower...or the hospital.

It was one of his fondest memories from their

marriage. *Hide-and-seek,* Kate had called it. If anyone had wanted to find them, they'd been hiding in plain sight.

And, if he didn't miss his guess, his ex-wife was preparing to help him find something *he'd* lost. All he had to do was meet up with Kate and her brother, then the three of them would find a way to help Alexa right under the FBI's and the APD's noses.

CHAPTER TWELVE

BLINDING PAIN.

She crumpled to the ground, taking her attacker down, too. Failure echoed around her—more screams for help, bouncing off the buildings that rose around them. Blackness sucked at her. An automatic pointed between her eyes. Pressed to her forehead.

"You stupid bitch," a disembodied voice growled.

The child's next scream ripped through her pain. Along with it came the certainty that it was almost over.

It was finally over.

"Do it," she whispered, the weakest part of her relieved as the alley finally faded to black....

"Wake up, Alexa," a warm voice intruded.

Her legs twisted in sheets. Came into contact with solid flesh...

"Ouch! Wake up."

She fought to be free, fought the pain shattering her skull, the darkness turning to gray. She'd left the lamp beside the bed on....

"Stop fighting me. You're not alone," the voice insisted. Her angel's voice. "I'm here to help."

He shook her shoulder.

She blinked through the pain.

"Robert?"

He came into blurry focus. And he wasn't alone.

The next instant, Alexa was up from the bed. It felt as if she'd left her head behind, but she was up and moving toward the door.

Falling on her face... Her feet still twisted in the sheet she'd dragged with her, and—

Robert caught her.

"It's okay." He eased her back to the bed. "Kate's with me. She brought meds and fresh dressing for your sutures and other things I needed from the hospital."

Kate?

A woman Alexa had never seen before hovered behind Robert.

"You both have to leave." She feathered her fingers over the surface of the bedside table. She couldn't have turned her head toward the light emanating from the lamp if her life depended on it. "There's no telling who followed you here. Where are my—"

"Keys?" Robert held them up. "You won't need them. We have someone outside who can take you wherever you need to go. Right now, lie down and let me take care of—"

"Give them to me."

She made a grab, missed the keys and nearly fell

off the bed in the process. Robert righted her but stepped away, leaving her personal space as quickly as he and the great smell that always came with him had invaded it.

"Please," she begged.

Had he said *pain meds?* At the moment, a hammer upside her head would have been nirvana. Lying back down and being taken care of would have, too. *Robert* taking care of her.

But she didn't dare. Needing it, needing him, was a slope she'd already slipped too far down.

"I've got to get moving." She explained without really explaining. "If you found me here, I don't have much time before—"

"No one saw us come in." The nurse—Kate—checked out the window. "No one will be looking for my car, and my brother covered us to make sure we weren't followed. In fact, his sources tell him this apartment is vacant. It's stayed unrented for three years."

"How…" Covered? Sources? Neither word boded well. "How did you find me?"

"Your friend," Robert answered.

Alexa shook her head to clear away more cobwebs. Wincing against the screaming pain, she finally got it. "Rick? He knew about this place? How… Why would he tell you?"

Robert sat beside her, and her personal space went out the window again. Kate disappeared from her line of vision.

"We've talked with Crimmons and Donovan."

Robert pulled a penlight from the pocket of his knit shirt and blasted a beam into first one eye, then the other. All business. Nothing about him hinted that he was affected by being beside her again. Touching her. "Actually, they did most of the talking. We know you were Dmitriy Andreev's nanny, and that Downing recruited you to help in whatever the FBI is working on with his department. Your APD friend wouldn't say much to me afterwards, but he's worried about you. So he told me where to find you."

Trying not give away a shred more of information than her visitors already knew, or a hint of how much she wanted Robert's arms around her, Alexa took the keys from his hand and focused on what Kate had said earlier.

"And your brother's a cop?" she asked, even though she'd already figured that one out. Couldn't pull one over on her! "Great."

She made it to unsteady feet and headed for the door, not really sure where she was going except away from the people whose arrival meant this place was no longer safe.

Kate stepped in front of her.

"Martin's not exactly a cop anymore," she said. "But he knows a few officers who can be helpful from time to time."

"I don't need any more help." Rick Downing had been more than helpful enough.

Of course, the bunnies on the other woman's scrubs probably shouldn't have been shimmering quite so violently. Hop-hop-hopping all over the place, no matter how hard Alexa stared.

"I just need to get out of here." She would have pushed past the nurse and the swarm of bunnies, except she couldn't get her feet to move again. "I have to make it—"

"Back to Evie?" Robert was behind her.

Alexa could feel his breath on her skin. His words, the shock of them, seeped into her, too. She spun to face him so fast, she would have kept spinning if not for Kate and Robert both steadying her.

"What do you know about Evie? Did they get her out?"

"Sit down." Robert tried to steer her back to the bed. "Then I'll tell you everything."

"No! Tell me now. I have to—" She stumbled over her own feet.

"You have to stop running away from me."

Her backside hit the mattress.

Robert's patient bedside manner had taken a definite twist toward cranky.

"I'm going to check with Martin and bring some things up from the car." Kate was out the door fast. Too fast.

Robert was sitting close beside Alexa again. Too close.

She wanted so much to rest her head on his shoulder. Too much.

"Crimmons and Donovan said only what they had to." He stared at the floor beneath his loafers, saving her from the temptation of looking into his eyes. "They tried to convince my boss that helping them find you was our best chance of caring for you medically. That the bastard you nannied for had hurt you when you tried to get his daughter away from him. That he's still looking for you, and that the FBI somehow needed a team of doctors to help them help you."

"And here you are," she observed, unsure of his mood. "So, now you're taking me back, is that it?"

"No. I figure the authorities were probably more of a risk to your safety than the Russian mobster they're supposedly protecting you from. You ran from them, and that's good enough for me. I was being tailed, but my ex-wife has always been smarter than I am, and her brother owes me a favor or two. So they helped me, so I can help you without anyone knowing I've left my house. You're safe with us here."

Alexa had grown so still, listening carefully to every word, dissecting what Robert knew and what he didn't, that she'd stopped breathing. He'd taken her hand without her knowing it.

God, she'd missed his touch.

"How much have you remembered?" he asked.

More than he wanted to know.

The bastard you nannied for...

"What makes you think I have?" Did Crimmons suspect the same thing? "What made you trust Rick all of a sudden?"

Robert pulled a folded piece of paper from the pocket of his slacks. Held out the familiar note. Waited.

She took it without opening it.

She couldn't look at Evie's drawing any more than she could look at him now. She'd fall apart completely if she did.

"How…" She swallowed, trying to clear the emotion away, to stay focused on the facts. "How did you—"

The apartment door opened inward. Startled, she nearly slid off the bed again. Kate bustled in, her arms overflowing with canvas bags and bulging plastic sacks. Her expression was cool, while she tried to hide her sideways stare at Robert sitting on the bed beside Alexa.

"Martin's going to stay out front and keep an eye on things." She set the bags on the table that served as the sparse, one-room apartment's kitchen counter. "I'll hang with him for a while. Let us know when… I mean, take your time deciding, but… Let us know what you want to do next."

And then she was gone again.

Alexa bit her lip against the instinct to call the nurse back.

"She's…" Robert waved a hand. "Kate means well, she's just worried about me. She's…family. A good friend. She'll wait as long as we need her to. She's one of a handful of people that I'd trust with my life…."

Just like Alexa had known she could trust Robert with hers, even when she'd run from his help.

"I…" She looked at him then, but he was staring at the floor in front of them once more. As if he couldn't quite believe he was there. He covered her hand with his, though, crinkling Evie's letter.

"We're here to help, Alexa."

Their gazes connected over his use of her name, her real name, for the first time. His eyes were troubled. Hers filled with tears.

"There's nothing you can do." She willed the moisture away.

In a few more minutes, she'd say whatever she had to, to send him walking out the door after Kate. A half hour beyond that, and she'd be gone, too. She'd given herself until morning, but that obviously wasn't going to work now. Once she found the strength to send this man away, she'd come up with another plan.

"You're right," he agreed. "I can't do anything for you until you're willing to help yourself. And whatever you think you're doing here, it's not helping. You didn't have to run from the hospital to get out of whatever the feds or the APD have you mixed up in. My friends and I will protect you while you heal. You're not alone in this anymore. Tell me what you remember, and we'll—"

"And you'll what!" Pissed, wiping at her eyes, she pushed off the bed. She steadied herself against the bedside table, just out of reach of the hand he extended toward her. "You don't know—"

"I knew enough to trust Downing when he gave

me the address to this place." He was her calm, cool doctor again, but he was also still *Robert*. Concerned. Totally focused on her, as if he always would be, no matter what she did. It was an addictive combination. "I know you're the kind of person who'll put your life on the line to protect a child. But—"

"You don't know anything about me." She pointed toward the door. "You have to go. Thank you for the medical supplies. I'm sure I can figure out how to use them myself. But you need to leave with your friends, before someone realizes you're here. Before one of you gets h-hurt because of me."

Robert stood, but he walked to the kitchen, not the door. "No one's going to get hurt, except maybe you if you try to run again. You'll never make it back down those stairs in your condition, and we both know it."

Alexa watched him unpack whatever Kate had brought, each motion deliberate. Calm and focused and unrelenting. Determined to fix things. To heal her. Except, it wasn't so much *her* he was trying to save, as it was the heroic victim Donovan had fed him a story about, so the SAC could uncover the information he'd wanted.

"You've got to listen to me." She sat back down because the room was spinning again.

Her stomach rolled from pain and hunger and confusion. As if he could sense what she needed, he magically produced a handful of crackers and a juice box from one of the bags. He even held the straw for her while she sipped. And that's when she found herself fresh out of arguments.

Robert had no doubt caught hell after her disappearance. But he'd come looking for her anyway. Him and a cadre of friends—people he thought of as family—who were watching his back, because he needed to help a woman who didn't really exist.

A woman who was too weak, who needed him too much, to walk away the way she should.

God help the man.

THREE HOURS LATER, Robert had sent Kate home.

Martin or one of his off-duty APD friends would be watching the quiet street out front through the night, in case someone else tracked Alexa down. It was an unlikely possibility, but since none of them really knew exactly what they were dealing with yet, they weren't taking any chances.

Robert had examined Alexa as best he could with the portable diagnostic equipment Kate nabbed from the hospital. He'd changed the dressing on her incision, given her an injection of a broad-stream antibiotic and watched while she swallowed a dose of pain pills. He'd almost had to hold the glass for her, her arm had been shaking so badly from fatigue and pain and maybe even the shock of seeing him again.

She'd fallen asleep the second she'd collapsed onto the mattress. He heard her shift on the bed behind him now, where she'd grudgingly agreed to lie down—for only a minute.

"Find out anything interesting?" Her voice was groggy, but it trembled less than before.

He closed the drawer he'd been peering into. An empty drawer, just like all the others in the unpainted pine bureau that took up almost the entire wall across from the bed. He turned, offering no apology for inspecting every corner of the apartment while she slept.

"What is this place?" he asked.

"Somewhere safe, in case I needed to get away." The word *safe* came out as a chuckle.

A very cynical one.

She swung legs that were swamped by oversized scrubs over the side of the bed and sat up.

"In case you needed to get away from Andreev?" he asked

She sighed. "Can you think of a better reason to have somewhere private to go every now and then?"

"Except you've never come here before."

She didn't waste energy denying it.

"There's nothing personal here," he countered. "No clothes in the drawers. Just a few nondescript things hanging in the closet. Outdated dry foods in the cabinet above a rusted-out kitchen sink that doesn't look like it's seen water in years."

"I never said this was my home." *Home* received the same treatment as the word *safe* had.

"So all your personal stuff is still wherever you lived with Evie?"

Alexa's blank look said *not exactly.*

"Can I have some water?" she muttered.

He crossed the room and extracted a plastic cup from the supplies she'd stacked beside the empty refrigerator—more temporary, throwaway proof that Alexa had never meant to spend any real time here. Turning on the tap was an experience. Rust-colored sludge flowed for several seconds, air pockets spitting until the water began to run a bit more evenly. Even then, Robert wrote off the plumbing as unsalvageable, and instead pulled a bottle of water from one of Kate's bags and filled the cup.

"You're dehydrated." He watched Alexa gulp the liquid down, then refilled the cup from the bottle. "It's common after surgery and the type of anesthesia you received. That's part of what the IV was for. You're crazy to think you can keep going like this and be able to do that child any good."

"You're crazy for being here." She snatched the bottle and handed him the empty cup while she downed the rest of the water.

The spunk in her reaction, the spark of life in her eyes, got to him the same way holding her soft hand always did, or having her look to him for help when she couldn't stop herself.

Evidently, there was nothing this woman could do that wouldn't get to him on a level he had no business exploring.

"I'm your doctor," he reminded them both. "That makes being here to follow up on an outlaw patient, after I spent so much time closing up that crack in your skull, my job—not crazy."

"An outlaw?" She snorted, then braced herself, her head no doubt retaliating. "Interesting analogy, cowboy. Does that mean you told off the sheriff back at the ranch, before you rode out to save the damsel who's too sick and distressed to take care of herself?"

Yep.

Alexa Vega, spunky and giving as good as she got. It was a turn-on he definitely had no business exploring. Now that the trappings of the hospital and the ICU were gone, and the memory of the taste and feel of her kept blurring the line between his personal feelings and his professional responsibility, watching Alexa *breathe* was a turn-on.

"What are you doing here?" she asked.

Good question.

One he'd been trying to find a sensible answer to, while he snooped around her rattrap apartment looking for clues into who she really was. Three hours of looking, and he understood nothing more than when he'd gotten there. Except that being in the same room with Alexa again, watching her sleep, had allowed him to relax in a way he hadn't since she'd run.

So much for *sensible*.

"I'm trying to convince you that you don't have to put your life at risk again," he said, "just because the Atlanta police and the federal cops are pressuring you to help them. The longer you stay away from Atlanta Memorial because Crimmons and his gang are waiting there, the sicker you're going to get. I don't know how that note slipped through the guards and into your room, or what the FBI is up to, but my staff and I will do the best we can to protect you from all of it, now that we know what we're dealing with. We have our own lawyers. I know several judges who could be persuaded to help fight Crimmons's court order. Come back and finish recovering."

Her shoulders rose and dropped, then stiffened, as she rallied to argue. He sat beside her and took her hand, ruthlessly using his touch to stall her long enough to get in one last shot.

"Whatever you think you can to do for Evie," he reasoned, "putting your life at risk isn't the answer." Her skin was so delicate beneath his, inviting his thumb to rub smooth circles over her palm. "However the police or Donovan or Crimmons let you down, whatever you think you need to do next, you're not in this alone anymore."

He'd said the same thing to Jacob the day his brother had refused to let family into his hospital room. *You shouldn't go through this alone,* Robert had insisted after sneaking back in. *I'm not leaving. I'll be here when you wake up....*

And he'd stayed by Jacob's side every second after that, until his brother had died from an inoperable brain tumor.

"I'm not doing anything for Evie yet." Alexa smoothed her free hand over the child's drawing he'd left on the nightstand.

"But you're planning to. Accept your limitations, Alexa, and—"

"Like you've accepted yours!" Accusation clouded her eyes. "Why are you so hooked on helping a single patient, if you're thinking so clearly? You're risking your job to be here, your career. You're risking your life, whether you want to believe it or not. You have no idea what you're getting involved in, because you refuse to see what's right in front of your face. For an intelligent, successful man of science, that's pretty shortsighted, don't you think?"

It was more than she'd ever said to him at any one time. More passion than Robert had heard in her voice since she'd been delusional—trapped between nightmare and reality and clinging to him for help.

Did she realize that she sounded more worried about *him* than she did upset because he'd barged in on her getaway? More worried about other people than herself? That was supposed to be Robert's MO.

"I'm shortsighted where you're concerned," he admitted. "Irrational and emotional and a bunch of other things that are really risky behavior for me. But it's worth it if—"

"I have to go." She tried to stand.

He gripped her hand and kept her beside him.

"I have to go," she repeated, but her thumb was rubbing his palm now. Her body leaning closer.

"Alexa," he begged. "Stay with me."

"I have a job to do.... I have to…"

"What job? You're a nanny, and you're too sick to take care of yourself at the moment. Get better, then you can help the authorities do what's right for Evie."

He cupped her head, wanting to tip it back and touch the softness of her lips to his. He pressed her head to his shoulder instead.

And Alexa let him. She was shaking her head, but she let him.

"You were out of your element when you ran last time." He stroked her hair, careful of the area around her wound, soothing himself as much as her. "What chance do you have against a thug like Andreev if you go back now? He's threatening you. Taunting you with his daughter's drawing. He may have even let her make that call to—"

"Let me go." Alexa tensed under his touch.

"Not until you listen to reason." He cradled her head in both hands and gazed into her eyes. "Yes, I listened to Evie's phone message while you were asleep. I admire you for what you've risked to help that little girl. But you've done all you can. You've got to—"

"Let me go." The desperation in her voice rocked him. "You've got to let me go."

No way.

"Kate's husband is a lawyer. If he can't protect you from whatever Donovan and Crimmons are after, he'll find someone who can. I promise."

"But Evie. She—"

"I have a lot of clout in this town. The APD and the FBI aren't going to get away with using an abused child to trap an innocent woman into spying for them. I'll contact the papers, the local news, until something's done about it."

She rested her forehead against his, their noses brushing, their lips brushing, hers trembling.

"No, you won't." She shook her head, her eyes squeezed shut. "You won't do anything. You'll go back to your sensible, heroic life, cowboy. And I'll go back to—"

"To what!" He gently shook her. "What do you think you can do on your own? You have to tell the cops what they want to know, then get out of this. You made a mistake. Took a job with the wrong family. And now you want to help a traumatized little girl, even after everything you've been through. That's admirable, but the best thing you can do for Evie is let the professionals take care of this now. You're just a—"

"I'm not *just* anything, all right!" She clutched at his shoulders. Shook him this time, silencing his next argument. "I didn't just stumble across the Andreev family by accident. Look around you. Think, *Dr.* Livingston. What do you imagine this place is? I had police and federal agents hounding me from the moment I came to your hospital. I'm not *just* the nanny, and you know it."

And he did know.

He'd been circling around the truth, ever since she'd made it out of the hospital—under everyone's noses, injured beyond the point where a normal person could have been capable of functioning. Ever since Downing had mysteriously confided what little he had.

Of course she wasn't just the nanny.

"What exactly are you?" he asked, staring at the stranger in his arms, a stranger who'd laid claim to his heart.

CHAPTER THIRTEEN

"CRIMMONS AND Donovan have intentionally given you a few misconceptions about me," Alexa hedged, not ready for complete honesty yet.

"I'm starting to realize that." Robert didn't sound ready, either.

But he was still there, trying to save her.

She laughed at the irony of her situation.

"Tell me what I don't know about you." Resignation weakened Robert's supportive smile.

How did she tell him and then protect him at the same time?

How did she watch Robert leave?

She reached for his hand again. She couldn't let go. He wiped a tear from the corner of her eye. Warmed her, as he moved closer.

Or had she moved?

"I'm an idiot," she whispered, her mouth brushing against his.

She reached for him, just like she had at the hospital. She sighed into his groan when he deepened the angle of the kiss and eased her into an embrace so tight she lost what was left of her breath.

"Alexa?" He tensed.

"Don't." She held on tighter. "Don't leave."

"I'm not going anywhere," he promised.

It was the same promise she'd made to Evie.

Evie.

Robert.

They were both going to be free, whatever Alexa had to do to make sure of it. But tonight, just once more, Alexa was going to take and hold and want what she needed. She was going to forget for just a little longer that promises never lasted, no matter how hard people fought to keep them.

Robert's lips trailed down her neck. His teeth nipped, his tongue soothing the bite. She gripped his shoulders. She needed him, and he was there, needing her back. They'd both be sorry in the morning. But morning was a long time away. She sank into the mattress, pulling Robert with her, groaning as the weight of him trapped her exactly where she wanted to be.

"Are you okay?" he asked.

"No." She teased him with a smile that felt real. Good. He made her feel so good. "You've stopped touching me."

His chuckle teased her back, even if there was still worry in his gaze. His palm roamed her hip, around to her bottom, fitting her against him perfectly.

"Better?" he asked.

"You're getting warmer."

She gave herself to the feel of having. Holding. To giving Robert pleasure and taking her own.

"L…" Her throat closed on the word, but she cleared it. No way was she giving up this moment. "L-love me, Robert. Please."

She braced for rejection.

"Yes," he agreed, instead of pulling away and demanding the answers he deserved. "Whatever you need."

She shook her head. "Where did you come from?"

His body melted gently into hers. His hands wrapped her legs around him. His lips kissed down her throat. "Let me make the nightmares go away, Alexa."

Hers or his? The raw emotion in his voice made it impossible to tell.

But she was suddenly certain she was seeing a side of Robert he never showed anyone. He smoothed her top over her head. His kisses spread pleasure, slicing downward to her breasts while she shoved her second thoughts to the back of her mind.

Questions and nightmares and responsibility and finding her way back out of this… It could all wait until tomorrow.

ROBERT NEEDED to go slow. Be gentle.

Alexa was still weak. She hadn't answered his questions. She was still in danger. But he couldn't stop holding her. Loving her. He feasted on the taste of her. The soft taut texture of her. Her body responded to every touch. One moment her kiss was consuming his groans. The next her teeth and nails were nibbling and raking their way down his chest. His abs. Lower.

Alexa clearly didn't want slow. Or gentle. Each of her out-of-control reactions begged him to let go. Forget healing. Forget protecting. Starving, he let himself need, maybe even more than she did. He rolled to his back so he could explore without crushing her. Alexa arched in his arms. His mouth returned to her breasts, his hands stealing beneath the waistband of her scrubs.

Shuddering, she shimmied out of her clothes, naked beneath, then her mouth was roaming, her fingers working his belt and the fastenings on his khakis until he was free.

"You're a miracle." He rolled again until she lay beneath him. Then he tore off the knit shirt he'd thrown on that morning, never dreaming he'd be holding her in his arms by sunset. "Alexa."

Love me.

Gathering her closer, trembling with her as they became one, he took refuge in her body and gave her his in return, knowing it wasn't enough.

Even though Alexa was in his arms, he could feel her slipping through his fingers with each passing second.

"YEAH, WE'RE FINE…" Robert was saying into his cell phone.

Alexa had woken to the sound of him dialing. She hadn't stopped him. She should have, but she hadn't. Because while she'd pretended to sleep as the sun slowly rose in the morning sky, she'd finally accepted what she needed to do.

There wasn't another choice.

"No, I'm not stalling." He was standing as far away from the bed as he could get in the tiny apartment, talking softly so she wouldn't be disturbed. But his absence had been what had first awakened her in the early dawn quiet. The loss of his touch. "She needs more time."

They both did. Except while the world pinkened beyond her apartment's cheap curtains, time was up.

"Yeah, I know." Robert turned, as if he could sense her silently watching. "Tell Seth I'll be in touch when I can. I wouldn't be leaving him in the lurch this long, if it wasn't such a delicate situation."

He closed the phone and stayed across the room. Trees fluttered in the wind outside, shifting morning shadows across Robert's face, concealing his expression. But his confusion was there. His reluctance to come back to bed, to her, stiffening the angles and plains of the body she'd memorized so thoroughly.

"That was Kate?" She found her scrubs under the sheets and eased the top on.

Her head resented the effort, but she swallowed the discomfort without comment. Of course, Robert noticed anyway. He walked to the medical supplies on the kitchen table and picked up the pills he'd given her last night. He was tuned in to her pain the same way he was everything else about her. Almost everything.

He brought the medication and another bottle of water over. She took both without comment. Swallowed like a good girl. Drank down the cool liquid. Shuddered when the back of his hand tested her forehead.

"You're warm." He walked away again to lean against the table and cross his arms.

"Yeah," she said. "I think I have a fever."

"I think you're right. I called Kate to get an update on things at the hospital. Seth's covering my ass. He's a good friend who was happy to suspend me so I'd have an excuse for being MIA, but…"

"But you need to get your friends off the hook soon," she finished for him. "Particularly since Crimmons had someone listening to every word you and your ex-wife just said."

"What?"

"Your cell phone. Kate's. Probably every call going in or out of the hospital right now. It's all being monitored. My guess is a sweeper team is already pinpointing this location. They'll be here in under half an hour."

"And how would you come to a conclusion like that?" Robert sounded as if he wished he'd settled even farther away. "What's a sweeper team?"

She scooted into her pants, then turned her back

on his growing suspicion, facing the headboard, shoving aside the pillows they'd slept on. Her solid oak bed was the only piece of furniture in the place not from a thrift store.

"A sweeper team cleans up the FBI's messes. My conclusions...well, they come from experience. Tapping into every phone call made by anyone associated with the prime lead in finding a missing person is textbook procedure." She pressed the hidden button disguised as a knot in the wood. "You snuck away, and the FBI thought you were still at home. Good going, except that the call you just made alerted them to their error. Any rookie would know that."

"Any rookie what?"

The hidden panel activated and slid to the side, revealing a safe set into the wall behind. Her hand shook while the scanner read first her thumbprint, then her forefinger. She felt Robert inch closer. Felt his shocked disbelief distance him more with each step.

She'd lied to him. She'd used him. There was no going back now.

"Alexa?"

The sensors cleared. The tiny click of the lock releasing echoed through the apartment.

"Any rookie what!" he demanded.

CHAPTER FOURTEEN

ALEXA PULLED her Beretta from the wall safe, along with its holster and her badge, leaving behind the assortment of other weapons that she could strap to various body parts so strategically, it would take a professional to detect them without a body search. Her nerves settled into a familiar calm as she felt the weight of the gun in her hand. Her breathing evened out. Her mind switched.

Click.

Back to business.

Then Robert sat on the bed beside her, his presence breaking through, refusing to be ignored.

"You *are* a cop," he murmured.

She closed the safe and listened as the lock reactivated. She moved away from Robert, congratulating herself when she made it as far as the table he'd abandoned. She sank into the lone, hard-backed chair beside it.

"No," she answered. "I'm not a cop."

Her mother had been a cop. A damn good one. The best there'd been.

"You have a badge and a gun and an apartment to hide out in and God knows what else in that safe. But you're not a cop?" Robert sounded like a parent finally realizing that his kid had been lying to him about drugs and girls and all the stuff teenagers did undetected, right under their parents' noses.

"Crimmons," Robert whispered. "Donovan. You're with them."

"I'm the principal on their team," she said. "At least I was, the first two years I was under."

"Principal?" he asked. "Under what?"

Wasn't it obvious?

"Deep cover. That's my specialty." *Had* been her specialty. "Profiling an asset. Finding an auxiliary way to infiltrate—"

"Infiltrate the home of a maniac like Dmitriy Andreev?" Robert was back to being a protective, irate parent. "As what? Supernanny?"

She waited.

Counted until she lost track, well past ten.

Her head was still killing her. Her mouth was bone-dry from the meds. Determined to make it to the sink, she only got to her feet before she had to sit back down. She distracted herself by checking the Beretta's safety, releasing the clip, then reseating it. Robert jerked at the crack and snap that accompanied her motions.

"The deep-cover operation was Crimmons's baby at first." She smoothed her fingers over the gun's elegant muzzle. "I started as a low-level IT tech in one of Dmitriy's legitimate financial businesses in town. Played the gullible but attractive genius with no common sense and money troubles that were easy to detect but not so easy they'd look suspicious. I got on his radar fixing a few high-profile bugs we'd planted. Waited to see if he'd bite. It didn't hurt that I fit the general description of what he likes in a woman."

"Petite and beautiful." Robert didn't sound pleased at the idea.

"Young," she spat back.

He eyed her up and down, as if he were picturing every inch of skin he'd touched last night.

"So what were you supposed to be?" he asked. "Twenty? Twenty-two?

"Seventeen. A high-school dropout, with a daddy complex." She stared at Robert, daring him to judge her methods. "Of course, we fixed my cover so Dmitriy would have to work to find out I was underage. He would have suspected anything that was too easy."

"So you were *just easy enough* to attract a pedophile, is that it?" Robert's eyes flashed cold fire. Ice cold. "What happened once he bit?"

She swallowed, then shrugged. In for a penny, in for a pound of flesh.

"I reeled him in like a pro. Donovan took over the strike team at that point. That's when things really started to get interesting." Her easy smile made her own stomach turn. "I was supposed to earn Dmitriy's confidence, make myself indispensable to insure my access to anything we could use to prosecute the son of a bitch. Map his illegal activities in permissive international jurisdictions back to work his hackers were doing here in the States, then bring the evidence in bit by bit. But if I could get close enough…"

"Just how close did Donovan expect you to get?"

"Not as close as I did." Turned out she could make it to her feet after all. She paced unsteadily to the door and back. "Seems I'm better at my job than Crimmons wanted to admit, so Donovan—"

"Figured since you had the most powerful, dangerous man in Atlanta under your thumb, you might as well play him for all the marbles?" Robert braced his arms on the mattress behind him and relaxed. Dangerously, deceptively relaxed. "A win-win for both your careers. So the whole nanny business was what—cover?"

"No." Alexa closed her eyes. Evie's tear-streaked face flashed through her mind. The memory of the little girl's screams while she was dragged away from Alexa. "Evie was never supposed to be part of it, but I—I…"

Robert was beside her. His hand closed around her arm. "Take it easy."

She was shaking. Her legs. Her entire body. But she was miles away from the bed and the chair. He led her back to the mattress, his expression unreadable. Once she was sitting, he took the kitchen chair himself, turning it backward so he could straddle the seat.

"I…" Her voice cracked at the amazing sight he made in wrinkled clothes and morning stubble.

A deep breath was all she needed. Except several deep breaths later, he was still too close. Close and looking at her like he'd never seen her before.

"I wasn't allowed into Dmitriy's inner circle that first year I worked at the downtown warehouse," she explained. "Dmitriy paid special attention to me whenever he was there, but no one but his body-guards are allowed close enough to know what goes on inside the Andreev home. Then…"

"The first year?"

"Deep cover agents can spend five, six years working an op until something useful is turned in the government's favor."

Robert gaze narrowed. Was he remembering her initiating their kiss at the hospital, right before she'd run and left him to explain it? Was he wondering if she'd worked him, too?

"How long have you been with the FBI?" he asked.

"Officially, since I graduated from college ten years ago." But she'd been a computer geek even then. And she'd been tapped long before she'd walked across the stage with her MIT honors degree.

And she'd been more than eager to serve.

"So this situation with Andreev, it isn't your first…*op?*"

Tired of beating around the bush—tired, period—she placed her gun aside and laced her fingers together.

"If you mean is this the first time I've been asked

to form an intimate relationship to get a mark to trust me, yes." She rubbed the area just below the dressing that covered her incision, trying to slow the throbbing that nothing had been able to stop but Robert's gentle touch. "Then I ran across Evie one afternoon, totally by accident. She'd…sneaked away from their condo in one of Dmitriy's cars and was lurking around the warehouse. She was scared, but wouldn't talk. I had no idea then… There was no evidence of what she was going through, so I…" God help her. "I took her back home personally. Used the situation to ingratiate myself with the child's father. She… Evie cried when I tried to leave…. Dmitriy asked me to stay and help calm her down. It turned into a regular thing, whenever Evie had an episode, until eventually my work was moved to the condo so I could keep a full-time eye on the girl."

"Donovan must have eaten that up."

Alexa ignored him. "Once I was living at the condo, I had a direct DSL link to all Dmitriy's operations worldwide. Within six months, I was working on key projects unsupervised. The nanny thing… It was always unofficial. Evie's very immature for her age and has no friends to speak of. She spends all her time when she's not with her tutors watching cartoons and videos. Her father travels nearly nonstop. And when he's home, he ignores her most of the time. I had no idea…what was going on between them. How sick he was and how damaged Evie's psyche had become."

"Her psyche?"

"She lives in a fantasy world, to protect herself, I think. I pulled her out of it when I could…. Got her to talk to me… I would have gotten her out of there months ago, but I…"

Some of Robert's anger deflated. "But you had a job to do."

"I was so close to having something big to bring in, and I was in a position to stretch the project I was working on indefinitely. Not that Crimmons was happy about the delay. He hadn't been happy with me for over a year."

"Why, if you were getting the job done?"

"I was doing it, all right. Becoming more a part of Dmitriy's world every day. I lost touch with my deep-cover team. It became harder to care whether I made my check-ins—even before I discovered how much Evie needed me. I—I thought… I was so sure I had it all under control…."

"The operation?"

She nodded, for the first time really seeing how badly she'd screwed up. "The op. The mark. When and where would be the right time to nail Andreev… To get Evie out, whether the team planned to or not. Crimmons was furious the last time I made contact. It had been months. I think the only reason Donovan hadn't yanked me yet was because I'd somehow managed to keep my cover intact while I found ways to protect Evie."

"By hogging all of Daddy's affection?"

"No!" Alexa snapped, Robert's assumption stinging deep. "Dmitriy liked being seen with grown women on his arm. I'm tiny enough to make him feel big and strong, and I'm smart enough to be useful to him. But ultimately, he didn't care about anything else—including sex—with someone a decade beyond puberty. So I did what I had to do to stay on the job, and to stay between him and Evie. So sue me!"

"And when you couldn't do both, you chose Evie over the op, is that it? Without cover, without protection, you tried to get that little girl out of there on your own."

He was coming close to sounding understanding again, maybe even a little proud—just when she was accepting how badly she'd messed up.

"Knock it off, Robert. My handlers gave up on me over a year ago. I got in too deep almost from the start. Made rookie mistakes. Deliberately didn't follow protocol. I almost torched the entire operation. What was happening to Evie finally yanked me back, but I should have extracted her when I first found out. Screw the op and how much I had to prove to my colleagues. And once I had no option but to run, I almost got her killed. I screwed it all up. I—"

The phone rang.

The apartment phone.

No one had the number but Evie.

The machine activated after a single ring. Alexa didn't have a chance to make it to the receiver.

"Don't think you can hide from me, Alexa," Dmitriy purred into the recording. "I found you at the hospital. I got this number. I'll find you again. You're going to finish the work you started for me. You owe me."

Alexa was hovering by the phone, holding tight to the table's edge. She didn't remember moving from the bed. Robert sat still as stone in the chair. Her free hand clenched in a fist, nails digging into flesh, to keep her from answering.

"It'll be better for everyone, if you come back, sweetheart. You…Evie… You wouldn't want me to hurt her, would you? You owe me, and no one leaves Dmitriy Andreev, Alexa…." The pause that followed vibrated with the sound of an in-drawn breath. "No one!"

She jumped when the line went dead.

The recording clicked off. Alexa could picture Dmitriy's trademark *peaceful* expression. He was always most peaceful just before he struck.

"Damn it!" She picked up the receiver and dialed, putting into motion what she should have back at the hospital.

She traced her fingers across Evie's drawing.

The call connected to silence on the other end of the line.

"The code is Alpha Tango 246," she said. "Clearance, mandate 1. Get Donovan on the phone."

"What the hell do you think you're doing?" Robert jammed a finger to the phone base, cutting the connection.

He ripped the receiver away.

She grabbed it and dialed again. "My job."

"Trusting the bastards who let this Andreev goon get to you at the hospital?" He pulled the phone line from the wall. "That's what you call doing your job?"

"*I'm* one of the bastards, Robert. Don't you get that? Dmitriy was *supposed* to get to me at Atlanta Memorial." She deftly plucked his cell phone from his pocket. "Even when I couldn't remember my own name, my job was to protect the team's access to Andreev's inner circle."

Robert glowered. She started to dial. He took his phone back with alarmingly little effort and gently shoved her. The backs of her thighs hit the bed, then her butt hit the mattress. He squatted in front of her, placing his hands on either side of her hips.

"And now that you do remember, after running from your bosses yesterday, you're suddenly ready to be their bait again?"

"That's my job!" She swallowed the pain of pushing him away. "I ran so I had time to think. But I'm going back in. I have to. And you have to let me go, Robert. You don't want me. You want the defenseless patient you thought you were putting your career on the line for. Your *innocent* damsel is on her way back to being a pedophile's whore, so let me go!"

"PATIENT? WHORE?" Robert wanted to believe he'd misheard her. "After last night, that's really how you expect me to see you? I know you're sick, Alexa. But—"

"I'm paid to think straight, no matter how sick I am," she countered. "It's what I do. At least it was. Open your eyes and stop trying to protect me from the choices I've made, before you're too messed up in my mistakes to get yourself and your life out."

Stop trying to save me, Kate had said countless times during her marriage to Robert. *I get that our marital problems had more to do with your guilt over losing Jacob than they did you and me,* she'd reminded him just a few days ago.

"Can I have the phone, please?" Alexa asked.

"No," was all Robert could manage through the jumble his thoughts had become. "You never slept with Andreev. Admit it."

She didn't say anything at first. Then she shook her head. "But it doesn't matter, not when—"

"Of course it matters. You're not just a patient to me. Not anymore. I don't care how long it's taken you to figure out you can trust me with the truth. You've put everything on the line to protect this city and a little girl. I want to help you. Stop trying to push me away by calling yourself a whore."

"The phone." She held out her hand.

There were tears in her eyes now, for the first time since she'd stopped being *Jane.* "It doesn't matter if I make contact again or not. As soon as you called Kate, my team traced our location. Cell phones are like GPS devices these days. You're just delaying the inevitable."

She was gone already. Miles away from him, and there was nothing he could do to stop it. So why was she still sitting on the bed they'd slept in last night, a tough deep-cover FBI agent looking more lost than ever?

"For the record." He pulled the chair closer, then sat again. "You're no longer a patient of mine, and not just because I've supposedly been suspended for obstructing a government investigation. But because..." Because saving *damsels in distress* was his biggest weakness? "Because I don't get personally involved with patients, and I've been emotionally tied up in you since before you knew where you were. And after last night..."

"You mean the sex?" Alexa sneered.

Robert crossed his arms, finally getting mad. He was losing more of her by the second, and for the first time in a very long time he wanted to hold on, not breathe a sigh of relief and let go.

"Don't play me," he warned her. "I don't believe last night was *just* sex for you, any more than I believed you could sleep with scum like Andreev to turn him for the government. I know better. I know you better."

"You don't know shi—"

"I know you're not just running back to your *op*. Something's driving you—something that won't let you leave Evie behind, the same way it won't let you trust anyone who honestly wants to help you. You've been fighting to get back to that child since I first saw you in the O.R. *She's* what's gotten you on your feet so quickly. What got you all the way out here, instead of coming clean with your bosses about your memory. Because you were planning to go after her on your own, weren't you?"

"Until you showed up, yes! You and whatever baggage *you've* got driving you. And now you're…"

"You're too sick to do this alone, and you know it." Still, she wasn't giving up. He'd never been more blown away by another human being. "But that doesn't mean you should trust Donovan and Crimmons again. Not just because I—"

"You're trying to help someone who doesn't exist, Robert. I'm not a victim. And I'm not a hero. I'm just a trained weapon that backfired on my handlers."

"Backfired?"

"I was under for so long, I wasn't sure which way was out. Crimmons was going to pull me, but then I stumbled across Evie, and the only way I could help her was to secure the evidence I'd been sent in for. But I couldn't even do that right. The whole thing blew up in my face, and now I have to fix it."

"And all of a sudden you think you can trust Crimmons to help you do that? You were set to hit the road again when Kate and I showed up yesterday." He took Alexa's hand. The connection was instantaneous. Soul deep. Just like the very first time they'd touched. "Donovan and Crimmons don't give a rat's ass about anything but nailing Dmitriy Andreev. Go back to them now, and you'll never make it out."

"Then I don't make it out." Her hand trembled, but her voice was rock solid.

And that's when Robert got it. She didn't want out. *Out* hadn't been in Alexa's plans from the start.

"Then I guess you're right," he conceded. "You're not the hero I thought you were. I fell for a fighter. I thought last night had maybe given you enough courage to trust me and what we feel. Instead, I've staked everything on a coward with a death wish."

"I guess so." Alexa grabbed her gun, then turned back to her safe and began fussing with the lock again.

Robert dialed Martin's number on his cell. Their watchdog needed to know he was off the clock. Deep Cover Agent Alexa Vega was suiting up, and her cavalry was about to roll in.

And there was absolutely nothing Robert could say to stop it.

CHAPTER FIFTEEN

"PATCH HER UP SO I can get her out of this place," Crimmons was saying to Seth when Robert walked into the chief's office.

"The *witness* you told me was merely your suspect's nanny?" Seth demanded. "The one you only wanted to question once her memory returned. Where exactly do you need to take her?"

"Let's stop pretending that your surgeon doesn't know the truth by now." Crimmons was in a controlled, lethal rage. "Or that Dr. Livingston hasn't relayed whatever tidbits of classified information he knows to you and God knows who else."

Robert casually joined the agent beside Seth's desk. "You mean you were stretching the truth a bit with that completely bogus story you fed us, when you were blaming me for Alexa disappearing? What a surprise."

"Look." Crimmons stared Robert down. "I don't care how you found Alexa Vega when we couldn't, or what the two of you did all last night when you were *observing* her condition. We have a sweeper team over there right now, sterilizing the place. Situation contained. But don't try and stall me or my operation again. You'll be putting Alexa's life and the lives of other operatives in danger. Just like every person you tell whatever you think you know will be at risk."

"*I'm* putting people's lives in danger?"

Crimmons pointed a finger in Robert's face, then visibly reined in his next comeback. He turned to Seth.

"Dr. Washington, I want this man kept away from my agent."

"Your *agent?*" Robert grabbed Crimmons's shoulder and spun him until they were nose-to-nose. He traded glares with the intimidating man without flinching. He was done flinching. "So we're officially dispensing with the nanny cover and moving on to what you really need Alexa for?"

"Why don't you gentlemen both have a seat." Seth motioned to his guest chairs.

Crimmons crossed his arms.

Robert jammed his hands into his trouser pockets.

"Sit." Seth had a succinct way with words when he let himself get around to being irritated. More succinct, the more irritated he was. "Both of you."

Crimmons sighed and obliged. Robert occupied the chair farthest away from the man. Seth took note of the lab coat Robert had donned when he'd stepped back into the hospital.

"Dr. Livingston is your *agent's* primary-care physician," he pointed out. "So—"

"No, I'm not—" Robert began.

"No, he's not," Crimmons chimed in at the same time.

"Okay." Seth waited.

When Robert made eye contact with his friend, something in his expression earned a compassionate nod.

"Okay," Seth repeated. "Dr. Livingston's suspension has been lifted, since your *agent's* admitted to leaving against medical advice with no help from anyone in this hospital. But it's within my discretion to reassign her case to a new doctor, and that seems to be in the best interest of everyone involved."

Crimmons made a rude noise.

One more snort, and Robert was going to—

"Is there something else I can do for you, Agent Crimmons?" Seth eyed the way Robert's fingers strummed on his thighs.

Robert didn't strum.

He didn't get angry.

He didn't fly off the handle and chase patients across town, sleep with them, maybe even fall in love with them, or contemplate the finer points of challenging another man to a fistfight.

"I need Alexa Vega medically cleared. Now," Crimmons said. "I need—"

"She's far too weak," Robert argued. "Too dehydrated and still in too much pain to do what you need her to do."

"And that would be what, exactly?" Crimmons asked.

"I'm assuming whatever she was doing when Andreev's men nearly took her head off."

"If she'd been doing her job, Doctor, there would have been no danger of—"

"You're really expecting me to believe she's been in no danger over the last two years—"

"I don't care what you believe—"

"Well, you damn well better care, if you want your agent released for duty anytime soon."

"I thought you weren't her doctor anymore."

"Not her primary physician, no, but—"

"Yeah, I'd say you crossed that ethical line last night," Crimmons agreed.

"Whatever happened is none of your damn business." And it wasn't going to happen again, Robert added for himself.

Alexa needed her job, period. Not him. She'd made that more than clear. But that didn't mean he wouldn't stand between the woman and these assholes using her up.

"I may have been removed from her case," he informed Crimmons, "but I'm still overseeing her care. Rest assured, I'll be the one signing her release papers, and that won't happen until—"

"Try and block it." Crimmons scowled at Seth. "SAC Donovan is waiting for results from our sweeper team. Then we're interviewing Agent Vega. There's nothing anyone here can do to stop that.

Trust me, Dr. Washington, you don't want the kind of trouble this hospital would have if someone tried. The federal government has a very long memory. Don't think—"

"Would you wait outside, Dr. Livingston?" Seth asked.

Succinctly.

Robert didn't bother disguising his smile as he moved to the door, closed it behind him and headed to the elevator to check on his ex-patient.

No one threatened Seth Washington and walked away unscathed, not even a federal badass like Crimmons.

THE NURSE HUNG an IV bag from the stand beside Alexa's ICU bed.

ICU still, because it was the most easily contained floor. Not that Alexa's secret wasn't already out to the only person anyone had to worry about trying to get to her.

The tall blonde in cartoon-covered scrubs Evie would have coveted began making notations in Alexa's chart about the readings on the monitors Alexa had been hooked back up to.

"Kate, right?" Alexa asked.

"Yeah." The nurse cast her the same worried smile she had at the apartment last night.

Last night.

Memories of being wrapped in Robert's arms refused to go away. The temptation to believe the crazy, supportive things he'd said before the sweeper team arrived. That he could really be everything she'd let herself dream he was.

Damn it!

Focus.

The cartoon-covered scrubs finally registered.

"You're a pediatric nurse."

"Not today." Kate's next smile came with a raised eyebrow.

"Because I need to be watched around the clock?"

"Like I could stop you from doing anything you wanted to." Kate flipped the chart closed. "Even with you dehydrated and running a temp of a hundred and one, my money's on you being the gal kicking ass if I got in your way."

"But you'd get there all the same, if you needed to."

Another smile from the nurse. Then Kate caught Alexa rubbing her temple, rechecked the chart and walked to a set of cabinets. She plucked a prefilled syringe from a tray, freed it from its packaging and lifted it to the valve on the IV.

Alexa caught her arm. "No more meds."

Too much was still up in the air. When it came time to confront Crimmons and Donovan, she'd be bargaining not just for her future, but Evie's, too. Unfazed, Kate pushed the medication into the IV, where it would drip into Alexa's vein along with the saline solution that had already reduced the room's spinning to a tolerable level.

"This is just something mild for the pain. And

without the antibiotics—" Kate walked to the hazardous waste receptacle and disposed of the syringe "—you won't be any good to anyone. You've risked serious infection, leaving the way you did. The oral meds Robert gave you at the apartment were a stopgap at best. Your fever's telling us something, Agent Vega. Listen to your body."

"The meds aren't going to keep me here when I'm ready to go. I've managed to blow this place once already." She sounded petulant.

Childish.

Like Evie, when she wanted to stay up past her bedtime.

"Yes, you did." Temper tantrums clearly didn't impress a woman who dealt with sick children on a daily basis. "But you'll only be hurting yourself and that little girl you nearly died trying to save, if you leave again before you can stand on your own two feet for more than ten minutes. Let the meds do their job. Trust them. That's the best advice you're going to get from anyone around here."

Robert's advice, and now his ex-wife's.

"I'm betting you being in here isn't okay with my handlers," Alexa said.

"The FBI didn't want me or Robert admitted back into the hospital, let alone this floor."

"But here you both are." Even though Alexa hadn't seen him, she was certain Robert was near.

He'd snuck under her radar, somehow, and he was determined to stay, no matter how clear she'd made it that she didn't want him there. What was wrong with the man?

Kate sighed. "Robert's got your back. And Seth Washington, our chief of staff, has Robert's. You're right where you need to be, Agent Vega, until you're strong enough to—"

"To make my own decisions?" she snapped at the other woman, sounding like a fourteen-year-old again.

"To have a fighting chance of crossing the street without getting run over." Kate's smile turned down at the corners. "In your line of work, I suppose you have to distrust people to survive. But if you were ever going to let someone in besides your FBI handlers, now would be the time to do it. I know how hard that can be, but I've watched the way Robert treats you…"

"He's not treating *me.*" If only he were. "It's never been about me. He's still treating Jane Doe."

Kate's smile went down for the count.

"Just like you putting your recovery at risk over one little girl maybe isn't really about *her?*"

"That's enough!"

Alexa's and Kate's gazes jerked to where Rick Downing had stepped into the room.

Robert appeared behind Rick, filling the open doorway.

"More than enough," he agreed.

Both men were angry. At Alexa for being so stubborn. At Kate for nosing into an already complicated situation. But they were glaring at one other, too, each spoiling for a fight the other seemed more than willing to accommodate.

CHAPTER SIXTEEN

"WE HAVE NOTHING to say to each other, Rick." The anger in Alexa's voice was for her friend, but Robert felt her eyes on him, even before their gazes locked.

"Then don't say anything." Downing stepped to the edge of her bed. "Give listening a try, Lexi. I'm heading the APD detail securing this hospital from whatever Dmitriy tries next. I'm not going anywhere."

"Dmitriy's not trying anything *next,*" she snapped. "You've heard the phone messages by now. You've seen Evie's drawing. He found me, even without you giving him my address the way you did Dr. Do-Good here. If he'd have wanted to hurt anyone, he would have by now. How did you track me to the apartment, by the way?"

"The phone number the girl used was routed through so many switches and stations," Downing said, ignoring her question, "there'd be no way to trace it to that dive apartment of yours. That's the only reason Andreev didn't come for you."

"He wants *me* to come to *him,* Rick. He needs me

to finish his damn project. Then he'll get around to making me pay for trying to take Evie. He's not going to mess all that up by coming after me here. So the lot of you can just relax and go away."

Robert caught Kate's rapt interest in the exchange. His own reaction was escalating to ballistic with lightning speed. At Alexa. At Downing. At himself and the entire convoluted situation.

"You don't know for sure how long the man's going to wait." Downing took Alexa's hand.

The casual, familiar gesture made Robert's insides clench, because he wanted to—needed to—touch her again, too.

"I know that Dmitriy's turned this into a challenge," Alexa argued. "He's showing me that he's smarter than I am. That he can control me from a distance. Now he'll wait until I do what he wants, which I have every intention of doing. You're not going to talk me out of this, Rick. None of you are."

"Or maybe he's figured out you were undercover. What does that do to your plan to push Crimmons until he sends you back in? You're not calling the shots anymore. You're not indestructible. Let the team in, Lexi. Let them help you figure out the smartest solution."

"The smartest solution? You mean like sending Alexa back to that bastard?" Robert took her chart from Kate.

Alexa ignored him, except for a flicker of a glance telling him to stay out of it. Out of her conversation with her childhood friend, out of her decisions, and most certainly out of the rest of her life.

Ballistic was starting to feel like a pretty tame word.

"Safe isn't the point." Alexa removed her hand from Downing's. "That's not why I took this op."

"No." Robert slapped the chart closed. "This *op* is obviously about proving something I don't understand. But I'm betting Crimmons and Donovan and the good lieutenant here do. Your *handlers* know exactly which buttons to push, don't they? And they'll push them. Whatever it takes to get them what they need. Your entire *team* needs a swift kick in the—"

"My operation team needs an agent that can close out an assignment!"

Robert caught the flicker of emotion darkening Alexa's flippant comeback. Honest emotion that drew Robert closer, the harder she tried to push him away.

Because he recognized bone-deep guilt when he saw it. It was the same black hole that had been driving him most of his life. Always circling him back to something he'd never be able to fix.

"Dmitriy wants me back," she insisted. "Donovan and Crimmons want their evidence. I want Evie to be safe. I'll work with the team, as long they agree to let me—"

"Kidnap a mob pervert's child, instead of focusing on extracting what you've worked for two years to collect on Andreev?" Downing gripped the bed rail, his knuckles blanching white. "You've lost your perspective, Lexi. I know you're working through a lot, and being deep under for as long as you were makes doing this by the book harder. But don't go back in, if you can't—"

"I'll do whatever I have to do!" Her beseeching glance toward Robert was a startling thing. "Please. Can't you make him leave?"

A fine sheen of perspiration coated her forehead. Her hands fumbled when she clasped them together. Not soothing her distress— not moving closer to her while the world narrowed to a few unforgiving options—was costing Robert. The anger that had been building since she'd pulled that damn gun from the headboard of the bed they'd made love in finally flared free.

"The patient needs rest, Nurse Rhodes." He walked to the door, yanked it open and waited. "Lieutenant Downing, if you'll come with me…"

Downing hesitated.

"Please, Rick." Alexa's fingers brushed her friend's arm.

Downing sighed and leaned down to kiss her forehead—a brotherly kiss. Supportive. Protective.

Alexa shied away.

"Lieutenant?" Robert repeated.

Downing looked torn, but he left and waited for Robert to do the same. Once Alexa's door was closed and they had the relative privacy of the hallway to themselves, the gloves were off.

"You owe me one hell of an explanation!" Robert stepped close, his tone too angry.

Too bad.

"Not here," was all the lieutenant said.

Behind the measured statement, heating Downing's hard stare, was just the kind of frustration and *give me your best shot* antagonism Robert needed to fuel his rage.

"You should have told me what was really going on when you sent me after her," he railed.

"Not here." Downing repeated, his fists clenching at his sides.

"For once, we agree on something." Looks like Robert was going to get the fight he was spoiling for.

So what if the lieutenant could tear him to pieces? So what if Robert was more pissed at Alexa and the runaway train she was about to jump back onto, than he was anyone else? He motioned toward the staff lounge several doors past the nurses station, then led the way.

Downing fell in step behind him.

EVIE HAD NEVER BEEN SO scared in her life. She dialed her father's office phone, Felix tucked under her arm.

She looked over her shoulder.

"Good girl," her father said. "I'm proud of you, Evie."

Her body was clammy, sweaty—even her feet in the Tweety Bird slippers Lexi had given her last Christmas. Her father had hurt her for calling the last time. He'd hurt her now if she didn't get Lexi on the phone. If she didn't rat out her best friend. Beg her nanny to come back.

So her father would have what he wanted and leave Evie alone.

That's what he'd promised.

Traitor! Felix's goofy grin screamed at her.

Run! Whatever you do, don't stop running! Lexi's final words in the alley screamed back.

She would know what to do when she came back. Somehow, her father was sure Lexi was alive, and Evie needed her. Lexi would understand, and she'd make everything okay again. She'd promised.

The connection started ringing. On the third ring, there was a noise like someone picking up, then a squealing sound that made her yank the phone away from her ear. When she brought it back, the recording was saying the number had been disconnected.

She's gone, Felix muttered. *She's never coming back.*

Her father smiled from across his office. He'd known all along. He'd told her Lexi was alive, just to get her hopes up. He pushed out of the coal-black leather chair that matched every scary shadow in the room where so many scary sounds kept coming.

"Daddy will get her back for you, Evie. Then Alexa will pay for hurting you this way."

"She would never hurt me—"

"You're only making it harder, darling. The number Alexa gave you, it's not working. She doesn't want you anymore. She's no good. Trusting her is just another one of your fantasies. Like you being in danger here. No one needs to save you. Why won't you stop—"

"Fantasies?" Evie jumped when his hand brushed down her arm.

"Your doctors said if you weren't getting better by now, we'd have to try the new medication," the hunter said. *This is Bambi... I need to speak with Thumper...* "I know losing your mother was traumatic, but that was seven years ago. You're fourteen now. Don't you want to get better? Don't you trust Daddy?"

New medication?

Her mother?

Memory flashed of a car exploding at their house in St. Petersburg. Evie being thrown back. Getting up. Screaming for her mother. Running toward the flames...

Screaming for Lexi at the warehouse and being dragged away...

You're only making it harder, Felix chirped, mocking her father.

Evie couldn't move, couldn't speak, while her father pulled a bottle of pills from his pocket. She'd forgotten what had happened to her mother. She wanted to forget again.

"No one's trying to hurt you here, Evie. No one needs to rescue you. You're safe, and I won't let Alexa scare you again. You have to believe me. Trust me. Be Daddy's good girl and take this. It's what you need, not your nanny. When I get her back, I'll prove that to you."

He held a pill out to Evie.

She shook her head. She kept hearing the squeal and the message saying Lexi had disconnected her number.

Bambi.

Thumper.

Her mother… Her mother was dead….

What was real? What had she imagined? Who *wasn't* she safe from? Was it really her father, or had she made that up, too? There were too many fantasies…

Always the same, Felix crooned.

When Evie looked at her father's sad smile, she could almost believe… She took the pill. Stared down at it. Had he really hurt her? Had she imagined it all? Was Lexi the reason she was scared all the time?

Evie didn't remember being scared before Lexi came to live with them. Before that, no one had expected her to be brave. Her father had taken care of her, and it had been okay to be numb.

She swallowed the pill and drank from the water glass her father handed her.

"Good girl. You have to promise Daddy not to try to leave again, Evie. Don't let Lexi hurt you anymore. You can't trust her, but you're safe with me. That's all you need to know, my darling."

I'm the only friend you have, Felix suddenly growled. *Don't trust him, either.*

Evie stared down at the stupid stuffed cat that was her last tie to her mother, hating him the way she suddenly hated Lexi.

"Always the same," she whispered.

"What?" Her father sounded so concerned. Like a real father, who'd never do the horrible things she'd thought were real. Like he'd never hurt her, just like he'd said. "Evie? You believe me, don't you?"

Evie blinked as the memories that maybe weren't real memories at all swirled through her mind. Felix started talking again, telling her not to trust anyone but him, because he was the only one who cared about her. Happy thoughts of her mom replayed, too, just like one of her cartoons—then all of it exploded, along with her mother's car.

Screaming, she threw Felix to the corner of the office. She didn't want to remember anymore. She didn't want to be brave. She wanted to be numb again....

She smiled up at her father. "I believe you, Daddy."

She'd never wanted to believe anyone so badly, not even Lexi.

"Good girl." Her father led her to his desk chair. Pulled her onto his lap, holding her close the way he had when she was a little girl.

She remembered being terrified of him holding her like this. But she wasn't so scared now. All the bad things from her memories were fading. It was the pill he'd given her. It was helping already.

Her father was helping….

She snuggled closer and fought to believe in the only thing she had left.

Her father stroked her hair.

"Daddy's good little girl…"

CHAPTER SEVENTEEN

"YOU COULD HAVE TOLD ME SHE was some damn super spy!"

Seth skidded to a stop beside the ICU break room. A crash from inside propelled him forward. He pushed the door open, then forced himself between Robert and the larger man his friend had shoved against the break-room cabinets.

"And you'd have done what, exactly?" Lieutenant Downing demanded, his face still in Robert's face over Seth's shoulder.

"Keep it down, both of you." Seth planted a palm in the middle of each man's chest and shoved. His friend kept struggling to get to Downing. "Crimmons has agreed to allow select medical staff in the conference room to monitor Agent Vega's condition, since we already know most of what's going on. Keep shouting details of the FBI's operation up and down the hallway, and I'm thinking that's going to change."

Robert tensed, then blinked at Seth, as if he'd just realized who had him by the collar.

"I…" He swallowed. Relaxed marginally. "Alexa's seriously considering going back to wherever she was hurt. And all this *friend* of hers can come up with—" he motioned his head toward the lieutenant "—is ten different reasons why she should work *with* her team again. The same team that set her up with Andreev in the first place, then didn't protect her."

"A deep-cover operation plan is designed to keep its principal agent safe while she completes her assignment." It was Downing who backed off first. He edged away from Robert and Seth, straightened his shirt, then walked to the coffeepot on the opposite counter. "Everything was in place. Organized cyber-crime crosses so many multinational boundaries, the scope of this project required director approval several levels above the Atlanta field office chief. The APD strike force I work on was pulled in to consult and provide local support. If Alexa had worked *with* her team instead of going rogue, she never would have been anywhere near that alley she was hurt in. But when it came down to it, I was the only person she trusted enough to call when she got in over her head…and I was too late…."

Robert resettled his own clothes. Seth sat at the break table and eyed the angry men now standing on opposite sides of the kitchen.

Robert jammed both hands into the pockets of his lab coat. "You got yourself assigned to Alexa's protection team, didn't you?"

"Something like that." Downing swallowed a gulp of the coffee.

"And you've known *Lexi* since—"

"Since we were kids. Our parents were partners on the force."

"Your father and hers were cops?"

"Her mother," Downing corrected. "Toni Vega was my dad's partner since they went through academy together. She was killed in the line when Lexi was just thirteen. Lexi hasn't been the same since. She feels responsible."

"How could Alexa possibly be responsible?"

Downing stared at the coffeemaker instead of answering. He filled two more foam cups, brought all three to the table, handed one to Seth and sat. He waited until Robert joined them to shove the third cup toward him.

"Our parents worked a lot of night shifts." Downing picked up his coffee, but he returned it to the table without drinking. "That left Lexi at home with a sitter—her dad was never in the picture. She kept begging Toni to switch to days. Toni and my dad argued about it—he liked nights, so he could be home while my mom worked nine to five. Toni and Lexi argued about it. Lexi eventually won. Toni asked for a transfer to another partner and another shift, and then—"

"No." Robert shook his head.

Seth could sense his friend's need to go back and save a vulnerable thirteen-year-old girl from where the lieutenant's story was headed.

"Within a month, Toni had been shot and killed,"

Downing continued. "Her new partner froze instead of covering her when they responded to an armed robbery at a convenience store."

"God." Robert pushed his coffee aside.

Seth watched the realization sink in. The connection he and Kate had sensed Robert shared with his patient. Alexa Vega was fighting to bring down an organized crime kingpin, because she hadn't been able to stop the criminal who'd killed her mother. Robert fought to save lives in an unforgiving surgical specialty, because he hadn't been able to save his brother.

"I'm not telling you any of this to make it easier for you to play on Lexi's emotions." Downing's challenging sneer was back. He drained the last of his coffee and crushed the cup in one hand.

"And I'm not *playing* at anything." Robert's anger was gone.

The lieutenant nodded slowly before continuing.

"Lexi came to live with us after that." He stared at the crushed cup. "There was no other family. She's like a sister to me. It's been…hard, watching the choices she's made for her life."

"You mean joining the FBI?" Seth asked.

"She couldn't just do the Bureau." Downing shook his head. "Just like her mother couldn't be *just* a cop to Lexi anymore, once Toni was dead. Lexi became obsessed with stories about her mother, and my dad was all too eager to sing Toni's praises. Every award or commendation Toni had ever won became larger than life. Every arrest. Every innocent victim she'd saved. Alexa couldn't just be a cop after that. She couldn't just be a federal operative. She had to be the top of her class every step of the way, even at Quantico, and she had to choose the hardest gig there was."

"Deep cover." Robert winced.

Seth wondered if his friend was rethinking the sacrifices that had gotten him to the top of his profession, to the detriment of practically every relationship in his life, including his marriage.

"And when the call came to clean up Andreev's syndicate operations in Atlanta," Downing continued, "she fought like hell to get on the team. They wanted a guy, but she's always been a computer geek, and Lexi doesn't quit once she's set her sights on doing something. She convinced Donovan she was the man for the job, over Crimmons's objection."

"Then you fought like hell to get your own piece of the action." Robert took his first sip of coffee. The next look he flashed at Downing bordered on respect.

But the lieutenant was still locked into his memories. "Like my help's done her a damn bit of good."

"It's starting to look better to me by the second," Robert conceded.

"No one with the Bureau knew she was leaving that day. She'd been notified that extraction was imminent. She was under the gun to pull together the evidence Crimmons needed. She was avoiding her check-ins, as usual. But then out of the blue, she contacted me in a panic. Dmitriy was leaving the country, only he was taking the child with him this time—without Lexi. She had two hours to get Evie away from the man, and she knew the deep-cover team wouldn't make the kid's extraction a priority…."

"But you would," Robert added. "And you knew Alexa was going to run, with or without your help. So you backed her up."

"She was in trouble long before that." The larger man was out of his chair in an angry blur. "She'd needed help for a long time, but she wouldn't let me close. She was getting more and more wrapped up in Andreev's world. But I wasn't her primary contact, so— "

"You weren't her handler?" Seth asked.

"No." Downing paced the length of the kitchen with the agitation of a caged animal. "The Svengali in this op was Crimmons. But I knew Alexa better than anyone on the team. When the Bureau started thinking she was going rogue, they came to me wanting my take."

"And you covered for her," Robert said.

Downing skidded to a halt. "I should have pushed the team to yank her back in sooner. But she was so close… I thought maybe if she completed this op, she could finally feel like she'd made a difference. The same kind of difference Toni had. Maybe she'd finally be able to move on."

"Close to what?"

Downing sat. "Evidence, for a federal indictment. Andreev's taking his Internet money laundering and banking fraud operations to a whole new level. He's working on advanced code that can strike several countries and jurisdictions at one time. Some new scheme he's cooked up to pressure his North American competitors out of business. No one knows all the details but Lexi. She was collecting date-stamped code and transaction trails. Proof that the source programming and project execution is headquartered in the States—because the U.S. is where he needs to show his strength. Andreev's been damn careful up until now. He's a legitimate philanthropist in the local business community. But an Armenian syndicate is trying to squeeze him out, and—"

"That's where Alexa comes in."

"She got a hell of a lot deeper than everyone expected her to." The pride in Downing's voice was unmistakable. "She's been working without a net ever since she moved into the bastard's condo. Everyone on the team, even Crimmons, backed off so she could take things as deep as she had to."

"Everyone but you."

"She was losing her perspective. Going for too much. The more access she was given to Andreev, the harder she'd push. She'd call me every few months, even when she wasn't making official check-ins. Kept saying she was close to having everything the op needed, but she wouldn't let the team extract her. There was always one more thing she had to dig out of the systems she was working on. Then the last few times, she sounded more focused—because she'd bonded with Evie. I—I couldn't tell Crimmons to pull her out. She had to finish this. She still does."

"Even if it kills her?" Robert began pacing on the other side of the table from Downing. "Is she going back to finish the job, or is she going back for the child?"

Downing didn't answer.

"Assuming she can get back in," Seth interjected. "How difficult will it be for Agent Vega to complete her assignment?"

"I have no idea. Donovan and Crimmons will debrief her. If she's smart, she'll be honest about the evidence she's collected and where it is. She'll have to work with the team to come up with a plan that won't get her killed, and teamwork has never been Alexa's strength. But good idea or not, it'll be hard for Crimmons to pull Alexa, now that Andreev's made contact." Silence followed, while Downing seemed to be absorbing everything he'd just said. "How sick is she still?"

Seth looked to Robert and waited.

"Any other patient wouldn't be ready to walk to the bathroom unassisted yet," Robert admitted. "Let alone slip out of the hospital, drive herself across town to walk two flights up to an apartment. Alexa's healing amazingly fast, but her body needs recovery time. Pushing too hard is already taking a toll. Her fever's only the first of many complications she's risking by not letting us take care of her."

"So even when she's on her feet again…"

"She won't have any reserves. If we're lucky, we'll get the infection under control and take care of the dehydration. But she'll be weak and easily disoriented for at least another week or so."

"Then the plan, if there is a plan, will have to be foolproof and fast. To have a chance of pulling this off, Alexa will have to go by the book."

Seth locked gazes with his friend and waited, while Robert seemed to be absorbing how much Alexa's recovery—how much the woman herself—had come to mean to him.

"From what you've told us," Robert said, "Alexa hasn't gone by the book for a very long time."

"No." Downing's expression was clouded with worry. "She hasn't."

BY THE BOOK, Alexa chanted to herself while Crimmons droned on and on across Atlanta Memorial's conference room table. *Take your lumps. Give them whatever information they want. Get the team on your side. Get back to Evie.*

Crimmons rewound the answering machine recording and pressed Play again.

"It'll be better for everyone, if you come back,

sweetheart. You…Evie… You wouldn't want me to hurt her, would you? You owe me, and no one leaves Dmitriy Andreev, Alexa…. No one!"

"He wants you back." Crimmons jammed his thumb to turn the digital recorder off this time.

"I'm the only one who can finish the final algorithm he needs in place," she said.

"Meanwhile, we have no idea if he knows you're an operative, or if he's just in a killing rage because his nanny tried to kidnap his child. But he wants you back. At least that gives the team options, which is more than anyone expected after that stunt you pulled."

"Nice to hear I'm still exceeding your expectations, sir," Alexa returned snarkily before she remembered to rein in her insubordination.

She needed a refresher course in *by the book.*

Dmitriy had first noticed her at one of his downtown offices, when she'd mouthed off at her supervisor right in front of him. She'd gotten herself fired on the spot for being an unpredictable troublemaker. Dmitriy had rehired her himself— because she was brilliant, he'd said, *and* because she was a troublemaker.

The off-his-rocker mobster had liked her spunk. Her sass. Which, of course, had been in the profile she'd carefully created for him. At first, Crimmons had been furious at the impulsive risk she'd taken— he wouldn't appreciate spunk if it up and bit him on the ass. Then he'd scrambled to advise her on how to play her new opportunity to its best advantage.

"You're dangerously close to exceeding my expectations for how thoroughly an agent can torch her career," he said now.

Alexa settled deeper into the wheelchair Rick had pushed close to the conference room table. Every eye in the room stayed trained on her. Rick and Robert were leaning against the far wall, side-by-side in some newly warped show of unity. Dr. Washington stood on the other side of the door. Donovan sat at the table beside Crimmons. The rest of the joint strike force, sprinkled in seats around them, wouldn't have missed the show for a month's pay. But no way were any of them stepping between her and Crimmons, literally or figuratively. She was on her own, same as always.

Only she wasn't.

She let her gaze fall on the men standing by the door, and accepted that they felt like more of a team than she'd ever let anyone at the FBI become.

"I'm your way back inside Andreev's operation," she reminded everyone. "Just like I got us all the way in the first time around."

She brushed her bangs back. The IV line feeding fluids and medication directly into her bloodstream pinched. Annoyed, she slapped her hand to the table.

"Take me out now if it makes you feel better, Agent Crimmons. But that makes you responsible for throwing the Bureau's two-year investment away, not me."

Eyebrows went up around the table.

Crimmons had all their careers by the balls, Alexa was responsible for the mess the operation was in, and she was daring to turn the situation to her advantage. Just like she'd been trained to manipulate every advantage she could get her hands on. Waves of anger and admiration rolled toward her. Crimmons sat smoldering.

He wouldn't win this argument. He couldn't throw her out of the Bureau until she'd outlived her usefulness to the operation, and he knew it. More importantly, everyone in the room knew it. All he could do now was give her enough rope to hang herself with.

"So what's your plan?" he asked. "I assume at least some of your reports were on the level. Are you still vital to the execution of an international money-laundering scheme?"

"I've never seen anything bigger. He has the access and the pass codes to online gambling and lottery sites all over the globe. Flushing his funds through them will leave Dmitriy's ill gotten gains as clean as a whistle."

As soon as she finished the final block of code that linked the intricate network of accounts together.

"And there's proof enough for us to nail him?" Crimmons asked. "Tell me securing that is more important to you than going back for this kid you failed to get out the first time."

Alexa controlled the urge to glance Rick's way. To snap that Evie was all that was important at the moment. To beg Robert to smile and hold her hand, anything, so she didn't have to go through this meeting alone…

All needs she couldn't let in, if she was going to play the game she had to play.

"The evidence is isolated," she said. "And I'd have gotten it out if—"

"If you'd waited for the team to extract you according to plan?" Crimmons asked.

"I would have waited, if there hadn't been a pressing need to escalate the timeline."

"That pressing need being rescuing the child?"

Alexa took a sip of water from the cup in front of her instead of answering.

Crimmons swiveled in his chair to confront Rick.

"And you knew about this when?" he demanded.

"A half hour before I arrived on the scene." Rick managed an appropriate amount of respect, despite his obvious hatred for Crimmons's bullying tactics. "I received Agent Vega's emergency call, contacted the extraction team, then headed out with APD backup. It's all detailed in my new report."

"Yes, including that by the time you got to the scene, there was nothing to extract but a near-dead agent with no evidence and no memory of what happened. Or was the amnesia part of your plan, too, Agent Vega?"

Alexa flinched while the entire operation team waited for her answer. She deserved the question, but everyone's calm acceptance of it stung.

"I didn't remember anything until yesterday morning," she said, "just before I received the note

Andreev planted. All I can say is that it was unclear when I first came here who I could trust, and I needed to think. Things became more—" she felt Robert's attention on her sharpen "—focused at the apartment. It's obvious how much Dmitriy wants me back. And it's equally obvious that I'm not strong enough to clean up my mess myself. That's when I contacted headquarters. I'm ready to do whatever the team needs me to do to succeed."

Crimmons threw down the PDA's stylus he'd been angrily making electronic notes with. "*Now* you're ready to cooperate. Now that both the girl and the evidence are nowhere to be found."

"They'll both be together, sir." Alexa steeled herself to play her one remaining card. "The flash drive containing the evidence has been with Evie for over a week now. And I'm the only one who can get to both her and it, before Andreev takes them out of the country. My guess is the only reason he hasn't flown Evie out already, is because he needs her to lure me back. That alone should tell you that my cover hasn't been compromised."

"And why is that?" Crimmons finally looked more interested than annoyed.

"He's obsessed about getting his code finished. Punishing me for knowing what he does to Evie and trying to protect her. He's acting like a megalomaniac and a psychopathic pedophile, not a mobster who knows he's been fingered. He's daring me to come back to the condo."

"So, once we get you back in—"

"It will be as simple as locating the child and sending the team an extraction code."

"Which you'll do, how, assuming you're not shot on the spot? It's not like you'll be given access to a telephone."

"No, sir, but I will be shoved in front of a computer and told to work on the source code that's held on a server in St. Petersburg."

"St. Petersburg?" Donovan's interest perked up, along with everyone else at the table.

"Yes, sir."

"You're compiling code across a high-speed Internet line to Russia?" Donovan pressed.

"No, sir, whatever piece I work on is resident on a computer at the condo, but Dmitriy doesn't take chances. I only work on a single section of the program at a time, and I check each section in and out of a code database every time, using new security parameters he gives me each day."

"Which means that—"

"Before I can begin work on the final piece of his project, I'll have to access his satellite hookup and download files."

"You're telling me Andreev will be forced to give you Internet access from his condo, if the bastard wants you to finish this job."

"Yes, sir. I'll be a loose cannon he'll want to eliminate quickly, which means I should be online within an hour of walking back in the door."

Robert flinched. Alexa caught the reaction out of the corner of her eye, and she let her gaze travel to him again.

In that moment, she selfishly let herself need him, want him, even though turning to him could only hurt them both before this was finished. In the midst of the mess she'd made of her deep-cover responsibilities, she could finally accept that she'd never stop needing Robert and the dream of him staying in her life.

The room had grown silent around her. The success of the op, her career, her health and her chance to make things right... All of it was on the line, and everyone there doubted she could get the job done. Rick didn't think she deserved to go back in, if she was going to blow things making another failed attempt to get Evie out on her own. And he was right. The only way the op would succeed was if she took the team with her. Trusted them. And she didn't.

She didn't know how.

Donovan cleared his throat. "You're asking me to stake the success of a two-year operation on the degree to which you've made yourself irreplaceable to Andreev."

"Yes... Yes, sir."

"Even after you tried to kidnap the man's daughter, you're still that valuable to him?"

"Yes, sir."

"And that's why he's threatened you, without trying to finish the job his men started behind the warehouse?"

"Yes, sir."

"Explain."

"Dmitriy can't get what he wants without me, even if his pride won't let him chase after me. He'll let me back in, because that's what he wants. He'll let me see Evie, because she's his pawn to controlling me. He'll give me access to everything I need to complete the op, because he doesn't have a choice, if he wants his billions turned into legitimate funds he can pour back into the organization."

Alexa let herself look at Robert again. His compassion and support, maybe even his love, were there in his sky-blue gaze. The same as they had been when she'd woken that morning. When she'd been so sure he'd walk away, but he hadn't. He was terrified for her. He thought she was wrong. She'd rejected his support every way she knew how. But he was still there, making sure that her last chance to do the right thing for her team and for Evie was at least physically possible.

He was still there....

Her dream within the nightmares...

"The question is," Donovan said, "can the operation team risk installing you back into what's likely a *made* identity, and trust that you'll follow the plan to get you and the evidence out?"

Alexa nodded, still looking at Robert.

"You've been under for years, Agent Vega," Donovan reasoned. "Overidentification with a mark while entrenched is a common stumbling block.

But, blowing an assignment this intricate isn't. If you can't work within the op's parameters, I won't be responsible for putting you back into the field. Especially since your chances for success in your current condition are already marginal. This is either a team effort, or I'm shutting the whole damn thing down."

Alexa made eye contact with each of her fellow agents, most of whom she hadn't spoken to in years. Her cover had become her life. She'd lost herself in Andreev's warped world. Let her mission consume her.

Except the world now had Robert in it. Someone to come back to.

"I think that's all we'll need from you for now, Agent." Donovan glanced over his shoulder. "Dr. Washington, if you'll escort her back to her room so she can rest, that will be all for you and your staff. My operation team needs to discuss our alternatives in private."

Alexa silently wheeled her chair through the door Washington held open, the truth finally sinking in. Her sass and the excuses and the rationalizations were all used up. She'd fought her entire life to be alone, and she was exactly where she'd intended to be.

"Dear God, what have I done?"

She stopped pushing. Robert knelt in front of her wheelchair. An amazing man trying so hard to understand her. To get her to let him in and stop facing everything alone.

"Please…" She grabbed his hand, like she had when she'd first woken up in his O.R.

"What do you need?" he asked.

"I need to go back…."

She had to go back. She'd promised Evie. She'd promised her team, when she'd first agreed to the operation parameters.

If Donovan gave her one more chance to do the job, to be the principal agent her operation team deserved, she had to be ready. And this time, she'd do the job right or die trying. Protect Evie from her father. Protect the world from a man who preyed on weakness and exploited every opportunity to do as much evil and cause as much damage as he could.

Then, when she made it out, if she made it out… Maybe she'd be able to make things right with Robert, too.

Maybe that dream didn't have to be over after all.

CHAPTER EIGHTEEN

ROBERT LOOKED THROUGH the open blinds into a sleeping Alexa's ICU room, except she wasn't really sleeping. She was hiding in plain sight, hiding from him, even though she'd reached for him outside the conference room.

He'd just heard from Downing—the deep-cover team had given the go-ahead. They'd be debriefing Alexa through the night, designing a plan that they'd execute sometime tomorrow.

She was going back in.

Kate turned from fiddling with Alexa's IV, saw him loitering in the hallway and briskly headed for the door.

"Get in here." She held the door open for him.

Robert turned his back to leave.

"Coward," Kate spat.

The APD officers flanking the doorway, one of them Downing, pointedly stared anywhere but at them. Robert headed for the break room, expecting to hear Kate's determined stomping at his heels. When he noticed she wasn't following, he whirled around.

"I'm not having this conversation with you in front of God and everybody."

"We're not having it, period." The toe of one of her sneakers tapped away, one annoyed beat after another. "If you're satisfied standing outside that woman's hospital room, staring through the blinds at what you've denied yourself your entire life, then go ahead. I'm just surprised you haven't pushed Seth to clear you for surgery rotation. That would be the perfect excuse, wouldn't it?"

"Excuse for what?"

"It would be vintage *Dr.* Livingston." His ex-wife's expression would have done a disapproving mama proud. "You'd have to focus on work. Back to your endless, faceless stream of new innocents to save. There'd be no time left to, say, face your feelings for the first time in your adult life and put everything on the line in a relationship with something besides your scalpel. Someone who means more to you than you ever expected her to."

"What's gotten into you?" The whole time they'd been married, throughout their divorce, he'd never seen Kate so worked up. She'd been nothing but supportive about Alexa until now. "I don't need this."

"You don't need Alexa Vega, either, is that it? I guess she was right—this whole time, you weren't really treating *her* at all."

"I was treating her!" He ran a hand through his hair and held on to the control he needed. The control Alexa needed from him. "I've never done more for a patient."

"And here I wanted to believe you'd actually let yourself want something besides treating and streeting every *patient* before you care too much about any of them." Kate looked ready to pull her hair out. "And the funny thing about our devious, coldhearted undercover agent Vega… I think she wants more, too, whether she can accept it or not. And I don't think the woman's let herself really want anything in a long time."

"Enough." Robert brushed past Kate. Then it dawned that he was heading toward Alexa's room, instead of away from it.

And *now* Kate was right behind him. He stopped. She skidded into him, smiling sweetly when he spun around.

"Back off," he said under his breath, feeling Downing's attention focused on them.

"No problem." Hands in the air, Kate moved away. "I spent six years perfecting that move with you. You know, back when I was one of the faceless victims you thought you could save, so you didn't have to commit to really caring about me, either. I think I've got backing off down by now."

Robert watched her go. Curbed the urge to follow her and leave Alexa behind and bury himself in whatever distraction would keep him away from the ICU until she was gone.

Vintage Dr. Livingston.

Alexa had trusted him to heal her. Last night, she'd trusted his passion for her. But now she was a deep-cover operative again, determined to work with her team so she could finish what she'd started. They were what she needed, not him, no matter what Kate thought. And he'd do whatever he had to, to make sure Alexa had what she needed.

She was extraordinary, and she was so much more than his patient. He reached for the door handle to her room and steeled himself for what he knew he had to do.

FIGURE OUT WHAT *you really want, then go for it. Then nothing can stop you...*

Alexa knew what she really wanted was standing beside her hospital bed, even before Robert took her hand. And when she gave up pretending she was sleeping and opened her eyes, she saw the same understanding in his soft, blue gaze.

"You can do this." He squeezed her fingers while he channeled her mother. He'd obviously heard the op was on. "You can do anything."

"So, you want me to go back now?"

"You have to go back." His voice touched every inch of her, making her shiver. The voice that had protected her when she hadn't remembered who she was. He would always be there, she realized. In her mind, whispering to her. Tempting her. Making her want him more than she'd ever let herself want anything.

His hand caressed her cheek.

"It's going to be okay," he promised, the same as he had that first day. "I'm not going to make this harder for you. I'm not going to be a problem for you anymore."

"You... You've never been a problem."

"Of course I have." There was guilt in his words. "We've just met, and I needed you to get better—for me. I needed you not to be in danger, because I couldn't handle lov—loving you the way I do and losing you."

Love.

Losing.

The words spun through her head.

She cleared her throat. "You... You..."

"Love you?" He nodded. "Yes. More than I've loved anyone in my life. More than I let myself believe I could. I've only known you for a few days, and I'm terrified of losing you."

Her solid, always-in-control surgeon. What had an admission like that cost him?

"You can't save me from this, Robert."

"I know." He let go of her hand then, when she'd always been the one to pull away before. "I'm not going to stand in your way. I'm not going to try and make you stay safe for me, instead of doing what you need to do."

It was exactly what she needed to hear before she went another round with Donovan and the operation team. So why did hearing Robert say it feel as if she was slipping back into her nightmare? She sat up to face him. To face the truth he was being honest enough to give her. Nightmares were her specialty. She could do this. She could do anything.

"You're letting me go," she summed up, her voice shaking. "You're finished saving me."

"Yes." He looked shaken himself. Then he did the most amazing thing. He smiled. And the rightness of it caressed her, even though he was several feet away now. "But you'll know where to find me, once you figure out how to save yourself."

She was too stunned to reply.

"Let yourself off the hook, Alexa." He clasped his hands in front of him. "Let go of your mother. Let go of me. Let go of all of the mistakes you think you've made in the op and the life you don't think you can have when this is over. Focus on what you need to do now. What you were born to do. But know I'll always be here, if you ever need me."

Always.

Figure out what you really want....

She couldn't stop the tears that came with the dream he was promising.

Robert was beside the bed again, even as he promised to let her go. He wiped the corner of her eyes and chuckled at the sob she couldn't stop next. He was offering her understanding. Acceptance. Freedom. Love.

The dream he was promising her was love.

"I'll be here for you when you're done with Andreev," he said. "No strings. No trying to protect you, so you feel like you have to break free. Just you and me, and the chance to figure this out for real. All you have to do is come back to me, Alexa. Trust your team. Trust yourself enough to get out of this operation alive, then come back to me."

"YOU WANTED TO SEE ME?" Alexa said to the smug bastard sitting behind the mahogany desk.

She'd been frisked at gunpoint and all but strip-searched. Her entire body was in agony from the strain of spending the last twenty-four hours huddled with her deep-cover team, and then dragging herself downtown, public enemy number one, to ring Andreev's doorbell.

But she was back in.

Dmitriy chuckled. "I always did like your spunk, Alexa."

"And I always did like you in that sweater." She motioned to the black leather club chair beside her. "You don't mind if I sit, do you? My head's simply killing me. It must be the cold front that's moved down from the Great Lakes."

Smiling, generous to a fault, Dmitriy motioned for her to sit.

"I hear you're a regular miracle," he said. "That knock you took upside your head—you shouldn't have survived it."

"The luck of the Irish, I guess," she quipped, tossing the hair that was living proof of her Hispanic heritage over her shoulder. "Your men certainly took their best shot."

"They usually do, when they know the price they'll pay for failing me." Dmitriy's next chuckle was a spine-tingling sound. "Suffice it to say, the men who let me down when they let you slip through their fingers are no longer in my organization. No one here will make the mistake of underestimating you again, Alexa."

"Sounds like you did a little housecleaning while I was gone." She inspected her nails while she casually looked about Andreev's office, scouting for signs of Evie.

"She's still here," he offered. "Not that Evie will want to have anything to do with you anymore. My daughter's remembered who she can trust, and after what you've done, she knows it's not you."

Alexa gritted her teeth against the knowledge that she hadn't been there to protect the child from this monster. She pasted on the nonchalant expression the operation team had decided would be her best beginning tactic.

"So, Evie likes you better than me, does she?" Alexa returned his smile. "Why don't you let her tell me that?"

"Why don't you shut your mouth!" Dmitriy shoved to his feet and leaned across his desk. "You tried to take my daughter away from me!"

"Your men overreacted," Alexa countered, verbatim from the script she and her team had worked up. "Evie and I were simply taking a walk, until someone could drive us back to the condo."

"There were police at the scene five minutes after you went missing!"

"Someone must have heard all the racket from the alley and called them."

"You gave Evie a number to reach you, in case something happened, when—"

"The number was in case we were ever separated, and she couldn't reach anyone here."

"The number was untraceable, Alexa. Then it was disconnected. I know you're a computer genius, and I'm just the man who's going to have you killed once you finish the code I need from you. But stop treating me like I'm a gullible fourteen-year-old girl. How long have you been planning this?"

Alexa ignored his fury. Keeping him off balance was key. He'd tell her more that way, and that would give her options.

"How long have I been planning what?" she asked.

"Selling me out to the police for child abuse."

She tilted her head to the side. If that was all he thought her break with Evie had been about, then she was on her way.

"I believe the word you're reaching for," she said, "is incest."

"How could you have been so stupid?" He sat back down, his accent growing stronger as his indignation rose. "You had my confidence, Alexa. I trusted you with my money. With my daughter. I made you a member of my household. I cared about you!"

"Yeah?" She twirled a lock of hair between her fingers. "I worked twenty hours a day, jumping through all your hoops. I took care of your clients. Oversaw your Internet activities. Your child. I was even okay with being your beard, hanging on your arm at all those stupid parties and events you thought were so important, to keep up your legitimate face in Atlanta business circles. I was fine with all of it, until I figured out what you were really hiding."

Sticking to the script, she added a sniffle and a shudder—neither of which were completely fake as she remembered the first time she'd known for sure what Andreev was doing to Evie.

"My relationship with my daughter is…special," Dmitriy conceded. "We became very close after her mother's death."

"Really? Because I got the impression that you being a pervert might have been the reason your late wife tried to run with the child herself."

"And you can see how well that decision worked out for her." Dmitriy smiled again, enjoying their sparring the same way he always had, especially now that she was letting herself sound more and more rattled. "You're a brilliant woman, Alexa. What made you think the same thing wouldn't happen to you?"

"I *wasn't* thinking. I was…" She shook her head, then patted the bandage over the sutures Robert had so carefully stitched into her head. *Robert…* "You were taking Evie away. I was protecting her, and—"

"I was tired of all your interference. Did you think I didn't know you knew?"

"I...I didn't think you'd take her away from me." Alexa called up the tears he'd expect. It wasn't hard. "I couldn't let her go. I couldn't let you hurt her again...."

"So you what? Decided to turn me in to the cops?"

"No! I panicked. I ran. Your men were all over me before we even made it to the street. I'd called the police anonymously, hoping they'd be a diversion, but   "

"Anonymously? They've been camped out at Atlanta Memorial for a week!"

"They wanted me to roll on you," she admitted, pleading now instead of challenging him. An intelligent but scared woman, breaking down just the way he wanted her to. "But I didn't tell them a thing, Dmitriy. By then I knew I'd made a mistake. I ran from the hospital as soon as I could, to get away from them."

"But you didn't come back here." It was hard to tell, but he seemed to be buying her performance.

"I may be overly attached to Evie, and I may have panicked, but you're right. I'm not stupid. I knew you'd never forgive me."

"No," he agreed, a sick glint of satisfaction in his eyes. "I won't, and neither will Evie. I've made sure of it. Don't even try to convince her to turn against me again."

"Does that mean you're letting me stay?" The extraction plan had contingencies for each possible choice he might make.

"You don't think I'd let you out of my sight again, do you?" Dmitriy pointed to the computer station beside his desk. "You'll be locked in here until you finish your work."

"But what about Evie? You're not going to hurt her because I—"

"She'll be fine, as long as you don't disappoint me again." He shook his head, a look of sadness clouding out the evil. "But you can't be her nanny anymore, Alexa. You betrayed her. You betrayed me. She doesn't want anything to do with you."

"But…" The moisture returned to Alexa's eyes. She couldn't help thinking about what Dmitriy must have done to his child to turn Evie against Alexa so quickly. "But I brought a gift for her, to…" She clutched the shopping bag she'd carried in. "To try and make up for scaring her the way I did. I know I shouldn't have done what I did, but—"

"No, you shouldn't have. My private life is none of your business. Evie's my daughter. *My* child! What we have together is none of anyone's damn business."

"I know. Please, Dmitriy." She put everything into begging the sick bastard. Whatever it took. *Execute the plan. Get back to Robert!* "Please let me see her. I promise I won't interfere anymore. I'll finish the last block of code for the project. Anything you want. Just please, let me apologize to Evie."

True to his profile, Andreev ate up every last *please.* He was reveling in the knowledge that he'd made her heel. That he had her back, exactly where he wanted her, and he hadn't had to step a foot out of his world to do it.

"All right." He flipped the intercom switch. "Charlotte, go to Evie's room and bring her to me."

He sat back to wait.

"Thank you," Alexa said obediently.

His regal nod turned her stomach.

They were studying each other in silence when his assistant knocked on the door and opened it to usher Evie in. The ghost of the child Alexa had left behind stood glassy-eyed in the middle of her father's office, a sweet smile on her face. Dmitriy walked around the desk to hug her.

"My darling, how are you doing today?" he asked. "I'm sorry I haven't made it by your room to check on you, but I've been a little busy with a surprise." He turned Evie to face Alexa. "I told you I'd bring her back for you."

Evie slowly blinked. Nothing else. No other reaction.

"I'm so sorry." Tears spilled from the corners of Alexa's eyes. She was still following the script, but every word was real. "I'm so sorry that I left you, Evie. I never meant to scare you."

The child looked up at her father, asking his permission to feel something. Anything. Dmitriy was too busy staring smugly at Alexa to notice.

"I brought you a present." From the shopping bag, Alexa pulled the stuffed animal Andreev's men had scanned and examined. "Something to help you understand. Something of mine from when I was a little girl, that you can keep, even…" The tears started falling again. "Even if I can't be with you anymore."

A flicker of recognition lit up Evie's expression. She reached for the stuffed rabbit Toni Vega had given Alexa years and years ago. Before handing it over, Alexa deftly activated the homing beacon she'd snuck in, disguised as the buckle on the animal's collar.

"It's…" Evie looked up at her father, then back to Alexa. "It's Thumper."

"That's right, honey. Bambi's best friend. I want you to keep him with you always." Alexa held her breath and prayed Dmitriy wouldn't guess the significance of the animals in the drawing he'd sent to taunt Alexa.

"I think it's time you went back to your room, Evie." Dmitriy summoned Charlotte again.

Evie glanced back as she was led away, but she said nothing. And that's when Alexa realized what she'd overlooked until then.

"Where… Where's Felix?" she asked once she and Dmitriy were alone. "Evie never goes anywhere without him."

"Felix?"

"Her stuffed cat. The one her mother gave her."

"Is that where she got the infernal thing from?" Dmitriy surprised Alexa by striding to the corner and bending down. He turned back with Felix held in a vise grip. "I'll make sure Charlotte gets rid of it for good. Evie doesn't need it anymore."

"She—she gave up her cat?"

What had Dmitriy done to her?

"My daughter's remembered who she can trust and who she can't." He tossed Felix to the couch. "She won't be keeping your gift long, either, charming though it was. You've seen her, Alexa. Now get to work."

Alexa indulged in one more look at Felix, then gingerly stood up from the chair and walked to the computer station. Her back to Dmitriy, she booted the machine while her mind raced through the checklist the team had prioritized.

Evie was okay. As long as she had Thumper with her, the extraction team would find her. And Alexa had Felix. Of course, she had a homicidal mobster in the room with her and countless of his goons between her and the nearest exit, not to mention that the world was spinning around her again and didn't show any signs of stopping. But she had Felix—the toy she'd sewn the flash drive into two weeks ago, when she'd been determined to get the evidence and Evie out on her own.

"Get to work, Alexa." Dmitriy returned to his desk to pull a handgun from his center drawer. "I want that code finished tonight."

Sitting in the chair, her fingers settling on the keyboard, Alexa ignored his threat and cleared her mind of everything but her mission.

All the items on the checklist were a go. Against the odds, completing the op successfully was not only a possible outcome, but it was also a likely one, just the way she'd bluffed Donovan into believing it could be. Despite every mistake she'd made along the way, she and her extraction team just might be able to pull this off. She just might get her chance to make it back to loving Robert, no matter how risky that dream was.

She watched the wireless router kick into session. Waiting for the high-speed satellite link to hook her to the Internet, she shoved aside the pain in her head and her heart, the exhaustion and the unholy mess the last week had made out of her body. She focused instead on the number of men Dmitriy typically had posted throughout the condo. The distance between her and Dmitriy's desk and his gun and the way he was closely watching every move she made. The extraction plan her team would immediately initiate once they received the encrypted signal she'd convinced them she could send, even if she was being scrutinized while she worked.

Dmitriy walked toward her. The muzzle of his gun pressed to the back of her skull. He leaned over her shoulder and placed a slip of paper on the table in front of her monitor.

"Here's today's log-in and password to the code database," he said over the sound of the safety being flipped on his Glock. "You have two hours, Alexa. Don't disappoint me."

Nodding, she went to work, logging in and opening a flurry of windows of programming code.

So many windows, so fast, that even Dmitriy couldn't keep track of everything. Settling into a routine, typing faster than she ever had in her life, Alexa entrenched herself one final time into the world she'd thrived on for too long.

Two hours, hell.

She wasn't going to need ten minutes.

Trusting herself, trusting the skills that had earned her the principal spot on this op, she was suddenly sure their plan was going to work. Her team *was* good enough to get Evie out. Alexa could count on them to make that happen. *She* was good enough to deserve this second chance, and trained well enough not to squander it.

She was good enough.

She had nothing left to prove.

Robert and his love and faith—faith enough to let her go—had given her that. He'd shown her she could want something, someone, badly enough, to find her way out of the darkness.

Trusting everything she'd learned about herself since waking up and not knowing who she was, Alexa called up one last browser window behind all the others. The one she'd use to fire off the extraction signal.

Dmitriy was right.

It was time for her to get to work.

CHAPTER NINETEEN

"SHE'S MADE CONTACT," Rick Downing said from behind Robert.

Robert turned from reading a patient's chart. He hadn't seen Downing since Alexa left yesterday morning, taking her FBI/APD joint task force with her.

"Is she out?" he asked.

The worry in Rick's expression wasn't encouraging.

"I'm not privy to that information any longer. It seems I'm too close to the principal agent to be a credible member of the team any longer."

Which explained what the man was doing back at the hospital, instead of off with Donovan and Crimmons and the rest of the agents.

"But you know Alexa's made contact?" Robert asked.

"I guess that means someone on the operation team is still too close to me then, doesn't it?"

Robert actually laughed.

"I guess it does." He clapped Rick on the shoulder and headed for the nurses' station to drop off orders for his latest patient's post-op recovery.

Downing fell in step with him.

"You off duty?" Robert asked.

"Yeah. You?"

Now why did Robert have the feeling the good lieutenant already knew the answer to that question? He handed over the patient's chart and slid his hands into his lab coat pockets.

"I am now." The double shift he'd worked since Alexa had left had been grueling, but he knew he wouldn't be able to sleep. "Seth and I are going for a beer."

"Dr. Washington?"

"We figured worrying together about how the op was playing out was better than heading our separate ways to brood alone." Rick raised an eyebrow. "Care to join us?"

He and Downing both had to let Alexa go. They were both trusting her to trust herself. To stick to the plan and get back out of Andreev's world alive. They'd both lose if she couldn't.

"Yeah." Downing held out his hand. "Yeah, I think I'd like that."

Robert shook, accepting that Alexa's friend had somehow become his, too. Another friend to wait with, while he was powerless to help the woman he loved.

All you have to do is come back to me, Alexa....

He headed for the elevator before Downing could read the anguish that must be written all over his face. The lieutenant's cell phone rang, dragging Robert back.

"Downing," Rick said into the device.

Then he nodded at Robert's silent question, confirming that it was about the op. But the lieutenant said nothing else. Whoever was on the other end of the line was doing all the talking.

Please, Alexa. Come back to me.

"YOU REMEMBERED ME," Evie kept saying. She rocked side to side in Alexa's arms, clutching Thumper to her chest. "I knew you hadn't left me, no matter what he said. I knew you wouldn't leave me. You promised to make the hurt stop for good."

"Yes," Alexa crooned, holding off the lure of slipping into unconsciousness. Holding on tighter to the traumatized child Donovan had personally brought to Alexa. "I promised. I came back. It's over, Evie. The hurt is over. You don't have to make-believe anymore."

"You remembered me. Thumper remembered me...."

Alexa knew she'd hear those words in her dreams for the rest of her life.

Dreams, not nightmares.

She'd made it out.

Trust yourself enough to get out of this mess with Andreev, and come back to me....

"A job well done, Agent Vega." Donovan squatted beside the chair Alexa had dropped onto in one of the Bureau's debriefing rooms. "I'm glad I got the team to see things my way back at the hospital."

Alexa picked her head up from whispering consoling nonsense into Evie's ear.

"Your way?" she asked. "You mean you're the one who—"

"Who convinced your teammates to send you back in to wrap this up? Yes. And I'm the one who held Crimmons off as long as I could, before he sent you the first order to extract. I believed in your abilities, Agent Vega, and your loyalty to this operation. Even when you weren't so sure of them yourself."

And because of the enormous risk he'd taken, Dmitriy Andreev and fifteen of his associates were now in federal custody. A handful of them would likely make deals with the prosecutors, once they saw the depth of the evidence Alexa had collected. Which meant the Bureau wouldn't just have a crack at shutting Andreev down, but the majority of his North American syndicate leaders, too.

"Thank you." Alexa felt the weight of the SAC's confidence settle on her shoulders.

It was a good weight.

"No, Agent Vega. Thank you. You've given years of your life to this operation, and your sacrifice has produced the Bureau's biggest Internet crime success on record. Regardless of the bumps in the road along the way, you're to be commended on a job well done."

"Thank you," she repeated, hugging the now-sleeping child closer while she remembered just how easily she could have destroyed the operation along the way. "I'm not sure Agent Crimmons is going to see things the same way."

"I'll take care of Agent Crimmons." Donovan stood and took a good look at the scrapes and bruises that were her reward for personally taking Dmitriy down, neutralizing his weapon and securing Felix while the extraction team took care of the rest of the condo. "Looks like we need to find a doctor to take care of you."

"Yes, sir." The memory of Robert's gentle touch garbled her words.

The result wasn't lost on Donovan. The SAC nodded and headed for the debriefing room's closed door.

"Good thing I've been in touch with someone who knows a doctor we can trust," he said.

He swung the door open. In the hallway, leaning against the opposite wall, were both Rick and Robert, both men smiling with pride and relief.

"You can examine your patient now, Dr. Livingston," Donovan said.

He walked past Robert, then shook Rick's hand in an easy greeting that left Alexa wondering just how much her friend had been *in touch* with the SAC over the last two years. So that's how Rick had known where her safe house was… Donovan must have known about her hideaway all along.

The pace of everything that had happened that day was closing in. The dizziness was getting worse by the second. But she fought to focus on

Robert while he took Donovan's place kneeling in front of her chair.

"How are you feeling?" he asked, his blue eyes and his warm voice every dream she'd ever need. He checked under her dressing and frowned. "I suspect you've done everything you could to tear out my sutures, but you seem to be holding up pretty well."

Holding up?

With him there, she suddenly felt like she could do the whole damn thing all over again.

Wait a minute...

"Aren't you suppose to be selflessly waiting somewhere for me to come tell you I love you?" she sassed.

She reached out and took his hand.

"Yeah," he said, clenching her fingers so tightly she winced. He looked over his shoulder to where Rick was still leaning against the wall. "It seems a mutual friend of ours thought it might be better if you didn't have to travel too far to get to where you wanted to be."

Rick nodded in agreement. He sent Alexa one of his trademark winks, then headed down the hall.

"A mutual friend?" She seemed to remember Robert being a breath away from taking Rick apart, the last time she'd seen them together.

Robert ignored her question, silently waiting as he smoothed his free hand down Evie's hair. He might have let Rick talk him into coming, but the rest, evidently was going to be up to Alexa.

"I got out," she offered, more afraid of her feelings

for the man in front of her than she ever had been of Dmitriy Andreev.

"Yes, you did," Robert agreed. "You and Bambi both. You're a hero, Agent Vega."

"I don't know about that...."

She thought of all the stories she'd heard about her mother, all the years she'd wanted to be just like Toni. To be off the hook for feeling like she should have been the one to go somehow.

And now she was a hero, too.

The word didn't fit. It didn't seem right. Not yet. Maybe it never would. The real hero in her mind was the doctor kneeling in front of her.

"You're a hero, Alexa," Robert repeated. "Trust me."

"I do trust you." She leaned forward as best she could, given the precious child she held in her arms. She kissed him, then smiled into his startled gaze. "I love you, Robert Livingston. You and every dream we can make come true together."

* * * * *

Don't miss Rick Downing's story,
the next book in Anna DeStefano's
Atlanta Heroes series
available in September 2008.

Love Inspired
HISTORICAL

*Powerful, engaging stories of romance,
adventure and faith set in the past—
when life was simpler and faith played
a major role in everyday lives.*

See below for a sneak preview of
HIGH COUNTRY BRIDE
by Jillian Hart

*Love Inspired Historical—
love and faith throughout the ages*

Silence remained between them, and she felt the rake of his gaze, taking her in from the top of her wind-blown hair where escaped tendrils snapped in the wind to the toe of her scuffed, patched shoes. She watched him fist up his big, work-roughened hands and expected the worst.

"You never told me, Miz Nelson. Where are you going to go?" His tone was flat, his jaw tensed as if he were still fighting his temper. His blue gaze shot past her to watch the children going about their picking up.

"I don't know." Her throat went dry. Her tongue felt thick as she answered. "When I find employment, I could wire a payment to you. Rent. Y-you aren't think-ing of bringing the sher-riff in?"

"You think I want *payment?*" He boomed like winter thunder. *"You think I want rent money?"*

"Frankly, I don't know what you want."

"I'll tell you what I don't want. I don't want—" His words cannoned in the silence as he paused, and a passing pair of geese overhead honked in flat-noted tones. He grimaced, and it was impossible to know what he would say or do.

She trembled, not from fear of him, she truly didn't believe he would strike her, but from the unknown. Of being forced to take the frightening step off the only safe spot she'd known since she'd lost Pa's house.

When you were homeless, everything seemed so fragile, so easily off balance, for it was a big, unkind world for a woman alone with her children. She had no one to protect her. No one to care. The truth was, she'd never had those things in her husband. How could she expect them from any stranger? Especially this man she hardly knew, who was harsh and cold and hard-hearted.

And, worse, what if he brought in the law?

"You can't keep living out of a wagon," he said, still angry, the cords still straining in his neck. "Animals have enough sense to keep their young cared for and safe."

Yes, it was as she'd thought. He intended to be as cruel about this as he could be. She spun on her heel, pulling up all her defenses, and was determined to let his upcoming hurtful words roll off her like rainwater on an oiled tarp. She grabbed the towel the children had neatly folded and tossed it into the laundry box in the back of the wagon.

"Miz Nelson. I'm talking to you."

"Yes, I know. If you expect me to stand there while you tongue-lash me, you're mistaken. I have packing to get to." Her fingers were clumsy as she hefted the bucket of water she'd brought for washing—she wouldn't need that now—and heaved.

His hand clasped on the handle beside hers, and she could feel the life and power of him vibrate along the thin metal. "Give it to me."

Her fingers let go. She felt stunned as he walked away, easily carrying the bucket that had been so heavy to her, and quietly, methodically, put out the small cooking fire. He did not seem as ominous or as intimidating—somehow—as he stood in the shadows, bent to his task, although she couldn't say why that was. Perhaps it was because he wasn't acting the way she was used to men acting. She was quite used to doing all the work.

Jamie scurried over, juggling his wooden horses, to watch. Daisy hung back, eyes wide and still, taking in the mysterious goings-on.

He is different when he's near them, she realized. He didn't seem harsh, and there was no hint of anger—or, come to think of it, any other emotion— as he shook out the empty bucket, nodded once to the children and then retraced his path to her.

"Let me guess." He dropped the bucket onto the tailgate, and his anger appeared to be back. Cords strained in his neck and jaw as he growled at her. "If you leave here, you don't know where you're going and you have no money to get there with?"

She nodded. "Yes, sir."

"Then get you and your kids into the wagon. I'll

hitch up your horses for you." His eyes were cold and yet they were not unfeeling as he fastened his gaze on hers. "I have an empty shanty out back of my house that no one's living in. You can stay there for the night."

"What?" She stumbled back, and the solid wood of the tailgate bit into the small of her back. "But—"

"There will be no argument," he bit out, interrupting her. "None at all. I buried a wife and son years ago, what was most precious to me, and to see you and them neglected like this—with no one to care—" His jaw ground again and his eyes were no longer cold.

Joanna didn't think she'd ever seen anything sadder than Aiden McKaslin as the sun went down on him.

* * * * *

Don't miss this deeply moving story,
HIGH COUNTRY BRIDE,
available July 2008
from the new Love Inspired Historical line.

Also look for SEASIDE CINDERELLA
by Anna Schmidt,
where a poor servant girl and a
wealthy merchant prince
might somehow make a life together.

REQUEST YOUR FREE BOOKS!
2 FREE NOVELS PLUS 2 FREE GIFTS!

HARLEQUIN®

Super Romance®

Exciting, emotional, unexpected!

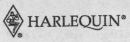

SAVE $1.00

A riveting trilogy from
BRENDA NOVAK

SAVE $1.00 on the purchase price of one book in The Last Stand trilogy from Brenda Novak.

Offer valid from May 27, 2008, to August 30, 2008.
Redeemable at participating retail outlets. Limit one coupon per purchase.

52608328

5 65373 00076 2   (8100) 0 11499

MBNTRI08CPN

HARLEQUIN
Super Romance

Lawyer Audrey Lincoln has sworn off
love, throwing herself into her work
instead. When she meets a much younger
cop named Ryan Mercedes, all her logic
is tossed out the window, and Ryan is
determined that he will not let the issue
of age come between them. It is not until
a tragic case involving an innocent child
threatens to tear them apart that Ryan
and Audrey must fight for a way to
finally be together....

Look for

TRUSTING RYAN
by *Tara Taylor Quinn*

*Available July
wherever you buy books.*

COMING NEXT MONTH

#1500 TRUSTING RYAN • Tara Taylor Quinn
For Detective Ryan Mercedes, right and wrong are clear. And what he feels for
guardian ad litem Audrey Lincoln is very right. Their shared pursuit of justice
proves they're on the same side. But when a case divides them, can he see
things her way?

#1501 A MARRIAGE BETWEEN FRIENDS • Melinda Curtis
Marriage of Inconvenience
They were friends who married when Jill needed a father for her unborn child,
and Vince offered his name. Then, unexpectedly, Jill walked out. Now, eleven
years later, Vince Patrizio is back to reclaim his wife…and the son who should
have been theirs.

#1502 HIS SON'S TEACHER • Kay Stockham
The Tulanes of Tennessee
Nick Tulane has never fallen for a teacher. A former dropout, he doesn't go
for the academic type. Until he meets Jennifer Rose, that is. While she's busy
helping his son catch up at school, Nick starts wishing for some private study
time with the tutor.

#1503 THE CHILD COMES FIRST • Elizabeth Ashtree
Star defense attorney Simon Montgomery is called upon to defend a girl who
claims to be wrongly accused of murder. Her social worker Jayda Kavanagh
believes she's innocent. But as Simon and Jayda grow close trying to save
the child, Jayda's own youthful trauma could stand between her and the love
Simon offers.

#1504 NOBODY'S HERO • Carrie Alexander
Count on a Cop
Massachusetts state police officer Sean Rafferty has sworn off ever playing
hero again. All he wants is to be left alone to recover. Which is perfect,
because Connie Bradford doesn't need a hero in her life. Unfortunately, her
grieving daughter does…

#1505 THE WAY HOME • Jean Brashear
Everlasting Love
They'd been everything to each other. But Bella Parker—stricken with
amnesia far from home—can't remember any of it…not even the betrayal
that made her leave. Now James Parker has to decide how much of their past
he should tell her. Because the one piece that could jog her memory might
destroy them forever.